Men look at me with [illegible] eyes. How I know their weaknesses! If their glances hold my eyes too long I flush and turn away. Stern old members of the nobility with their voices talking of empire and glory would like nothing more than to be naked at my feet. I have toyed with such before. I have had them kneeling and licking between my toes while I assumed an expression of languid boredom and disinterest.

NINA FOXTON

Titian Beresford

MASQUERADE BOOKS, INC.
801 SECOND AVENUE
NEW YORK, N.Y. 10017

Any resemblance between persons, places or events within the work "Nina Foxton" and actual persons, places or events, past, present or future is purely coincidental and shall in no way be construed to be intentional. "Nina Foxton" is simply a work of fiction written only for fantasy entertainment

First Masquerade Edition 1991

First printing July 1991

ISBN 1-878320-70-X

Manufactured in the United States of America
Published by Masquerade Books, Inc.
801 Second Avenue
New York, N.Y. 10017

For those whose intellect may true divine
The difference between the truth sublime,
And fantasy, however fair
Is still akin to empty air.
Some dreams that shine so fair in thought
Should ne'er into this world be brought.
Enjoy this sumptuous fictional feast,
For sensory delights are not the least.
But do not try with wayward heart
To breathe it life lest chaos start.

To each its own realm, no crossing be
Twixt fantasy worlds and reality.

CHAPTER I

The London train puffs like an old gentleman after fine cigars and sherry. My boredom increases as I gaze out from the windows at meadows bright with spring flowers. The trees retain the youthful green of new leaves rejoicing at their freedom from the confines of their buds. White clouds move imperceptibly in a sky of clearest blue. Annoyed with my boredom I concentrate rather on the dust that lies on the quilted windowsill. My coach is stuffy but I would not open the window to brave the soot. I slip out of my kidskin boots and crossing my ankles demurely rest my silk-stockinged feet on the seat across from me. From my bag I withdraw the packet containing the letters from my aunt. I open the latest one and read. It is but a note.

Dearest Nina.

I must again apologize for not being at Wellingham to welcome you. I am sure that you will find Oxfordshire much to your liking. I have instructed Sir Albert as to the time of your arrival and he will be at the Chalgrove station with a carriage to meet you at the appointed hour. We are well here. The Massoun estate is on the Loire. What parties we have! I do wish you could be along. I'm not sure how long I will remain as Lisette is quite desperate for me to stay yet awhile. At any rate, the house is at your disposal. With regards and love,

Aunt Judith

The compartment door opens. A conductor inquires if I would object to others entering. The train is crowded, he says. All the while his eyes are on my breasts. Then they drop to my hips...and lower still. I spread my legs slightly. He knows his place. Does he know I would have him under me? Does he know that I would love to order him about? To see his moustache twitch with stifled words he dare not say in reply to my imperious haughty commands would be a lark. To have his undoubtedly hot cock drilling into me would be another. I nod. I will allow it because often when I am bored others amuse me. As the door closes I slip into my boots and put the letters away.

The first other passenger to enter is a man of middle years and well dressed. A vicar perhaps, or a doctor…no, I think not. A vicar it is. His eyes scurry from mine as we exchange pleasantries. Occasionally they dart furtively about my person to linger in unguarded moments on my hips and breasts. I ignore him and study my lace gloves. With my fingertip I flick a mote of dust from the quilting.

Moments later the peace of the compartment is shattered. A young lady enters practically dragging a squealing red-faced boy. She is his sister. Her eyes speak apologies for his clamor. The vicar moves beside me to allow them to have the facing seat. How generous he is. As they settle down after stowing their bags in the overhead racks the girl speaks. They have come from the coast she says. A very long day. A hot day to travel.

The boy continues his tantrum. I would thrash him at once. A thrashing he would not soon forget. I see in the vicar's eyes the same sentiments. I look back at the girl and reply my understanding. It is a very hot day to travel, though a fine one nonetheless. We speak of fashion. Of what they wear in Paris. I don't care for Paris, though I reply in kind. Meaningless words between strangers on a train. Silly pleasantries.

I soon grow bored again. The girl is silly and flits like a butterfly from thought to thought. There is no strictness in her. The boy has no fear of her whatsoever. He has his way. Were he my brother there would be fear of me in him, I would see to it. While the vicar keeps glancing at me now and again and the girl chatters on about bustles, my mind is active. While my lips make polite noises my mind works on a solution to the boredom.

It would be great fun to paddle the boy and lick the tight little pussy of the girl. I will at least arrange the former. The boy's behavior is atrocious. He sits and fidgets, rolling his eyes. Now and again he reaches over to pinch his sister's hip. He bangs his heels on the wooden scroll-work beneath the seat cushion. The vicar gives the boy what he imagines is a withering glance. The boy sticks out his tongue and pulls at the lace on his sister's dress. The vicar is a man of hopeless conceit. I encourage the boy. I smile as his fingers pull at his sister's lace. He does it again only this time harder. He winks at me and his sister's lace tears. She shouts at him with tears in her eyes. "George! How could you do such a beastly thing! You have ruined my dress. You have been acting just awfully. Now what am I going to do?" She goes on and on with a veritable dirge about her dress. The vicar mumbles his sympathy and tries again to stifle the boy with a glance of godlike authority. I speak then. The time is proper and an end to my boredom is in sight.

"I am by profession a governess and much experienced in curbing wayward impulses within the young. I am sorry to say that your brother desperately needs a caning. A caning properly administered by a knowing and skillful hand could do a great deal to alleviate your present burden. It would turn this rascal into a young gentleman and make the rest of your trip lightsome and easy compared to what it has been."

The vicar nods his approval.

The young woman inquires, "Have you a cane, Miss?"

The boy squirms now in growing alarm.

"I have no cane, however I am certain that a strap from one of the bags overhead would most admirably serve the purpose." The young lady stands up, and assisted by the ever-so-gallant vicar, she obtains the leather strap.

The leather is supple and fine and I look forward to putting it to good use. "Now if you please, perhaps you could take down the young man's trousers. He may then be laid across the seat where he now sits."

The boy's sister, again with aid from the vicar, does as I request. I then indicate to her that I am going to stand to carry out the strapping and suggest she sit in my seat to watch. She does so, evidently much relieved that someone is taking her brother in hand. The white bottom of the boy—now fully exposed—begins to flex nervously and he gasps out his too-late apologies. He is determined not to blubber. I can tell that by the set of his jaw. He is going to play the man. I am amused. Standing between the seats I bend over slightly at the waist to get a good angle with the strap. My bottom is thus thrust nearly into the vicar's face.

I am sure the vicar is not watching the strapping. His mind is now on other things, such as the desire the proximity of my shapely bottomcheeks has stirred in him. I bring the strap down across the boy's backside. It lands with a loud crack. I continue. I feel my face flush as my arm takes up the familiar rhythm. Over and over again I bring down the strap. At a command from me the sister leans forward to hold her brother's arms. She holds him still. There is satisfaction in her eyes. The boy has lost all pretence now. He is shameless in his blubbering. I take my task very seriously. He is now quite beside himself. His bottom is crimson and ripples from the force of each blow; my strokes even begin to move down the backs of his thighs. At last the vicar tenses behind me. Even the girl's eyes are almost ready to question. After giving one extra hard stroke for good measure, I cease. I would have gone on. The boy is not yet broken, though his wails are pathetic and loud. However, the strong must at times make allowances for the sensibilities of the weak. I am all aquiver with the enjoyment of it. I can feel the wetness spreading between my thighs, urging me to attempt additional liberties with my new companions.

Before I can do so, however, the much-humbled brother and his sister leave the train. A small country station. I can tell the young man on the water tower is furnished with a long, thick cock that would provide the relief I need. I want to feel him hot in my hand. When he looks in my direction I turn away, a proper lady of discretion.

The vicar and I are alone now. I have the measure of him. It is an amusement to know where the puppet strings are. It is an amusement to know how to make the puppets dance. I tell the vicar that it is a pity.

"What is a pity, Miss?"

"Why, the loss of your position; the loss of your home in the vicarage and the disgrace of course."

His eyes widen and his face pales. "Whatever can you mean?"

"Well, when it becomes known that you did not carry yourself with the proper deportment of a man of stature. The lewd suggestions, the grasping and pinching. You are a very wicked man." I have him now. He is my obedient servant. He understands his predicament. He knows that I am his master. I fasten the door. I go back and sit beside him. I stroke his hair and smile with disdain. He is trembling now. He does not know what to expect. He should know. The males are truly the weak sex. Rob them of their seed and they are gelded. Hold out to them the promise of such gelding and they are fawning puppies. They amuse me. No woman would ever consent to such handling. Only the male delights in the submission. If ever a woman submits it is for a purpose. A purpose of her own.

I tell the vicar that he must be naked. He jumps at the snap of my command. I have the understanding of command. My eyes and my voice can be like whips when I so choose. The vicar is so obedient that I am merciful. I tell him that he may leave on his shirt, which barely covers his buttocks. I have him stand and turn before me. His mouth twitches. His flanks are pale. His sac is heavy with his balls clearly outlined within. His penis lolls downward as if blushing, still hooded by his foreskin.

I am coy. I maintain an air of proper reservation. As if I am undertaking a scientific study. I act coolly curious. I slip off my gloves. I want to feel him in my bare hand. I lightly touch his bottom. His manhood stirs. Then my fingers gently grip his sac. His penis slowly twitches to a full state of urgent arousal. I grasp it and pull back the hood to expose the head, dark and swollen. There is pleading in his eyes. My eyes remain casual and bored. I have him kneel before me. His penis is thoroughly engorged and stands out from his belly like a lance. I ask him if he wouldn't be a gentleman and take off my boots. He does so with reverence. The vicar understands reverence. I wiggle my toes.

I stroke his face with one foot while with the other I

press his penis back against his abdomen. I work him with my toes. An idea strikes me. Another amusement lends itself. We are about to pass a small station without stopping. I have the vicar kneel on the seat facing the window.

The train slows. I open the shade on the window until the vicar's front shows from chin to thigh. His bouncing cock is plainly visible. I put my gloves back on and stand behind him. I reach around, grab his shaft, and pump him gently as the train goes past the platform. I can imagine it. In the window a swollen penis and a woman's gloved hand working it. The people stare stupidly. I laugh as he trembles.

I work him until we are in the countryside again. "No, silly, they could not see your face." He is at his wit's end. I have him turn around and stand. He must lace his fingers behind his head. I sit beside him. I grasp him and lure my fingers up and down the length of his fat sausage. I skin him up and down. I want to see his spurting. I work him steadily. He moans and shuts his eyes. I bring the palm of my hand over his cockhead, then run my fingers down the shaft to his balls. I linger there a moment before continuing the masturbatory motion...only harder this time, much harder. His breath comes in ragged little gasps now. With my foot I draw over the pile of his clothes. I hold the vicar's penis as it spurts. I point it at his clothes. It swells and jumps in my gloved hand. Thick drops shower all over his trousers and his jacket. I laugh. I spray his clothes with his erupting seed. How amusing he is. What a delight it is to handle a swollen spurting penis.

Afterward he sits dressed with his face crimson. The residue of his orgasm is are still plainly visible. He tries to hide it with his bag. The train arrives in Chalgrove. The vicar's hands are shaking. I laugh. How he amuses me. Of course I have him play the gentleman. A poor stuttering vicar with wet spots on his trousers and jacket carries my things off the train. How people stare. I stand with the cart that holds my luggage. The vicar slinks away. I wait for Sir Albert. The porters stroke me with their eyes. They would like nothing better than to fuck me.

I shade myself with my parasol. I twirl it slowly and

pivot my boot on the boards of the platform. Sir Albert is late. I am annoyed, yet I will not show him my displeasure. First I must take his measure. I must find out where his strings are. A puppeteer must first find the strings. People hurry to and fro. One young woman catches my eye. She has regal bearing and the assurance that comes with control. I can see it in her eyes. A glance of mutual respect passes between us. The man who escorts her is attentive. I imagine how she controls him for I delight in imagining such things. As a reward when he is obedient he must feel the softness of her hands gently goading his swollen prick. The silly prick that swells with the urge to shame itself. The silly prick so eager to soil a woman's hands. I smile at the thought of it. A young porter passes me. He thinks my smile is for him and blushes crimson. I would have him licking me. His mouth nursing at my cunt. I would like the tip to probe inside my slit and scour the smooth inner membranes. Then I wish it to stab me like a miniature penis until I flood his mouth with my come. How males thirst for such things. Such dalliances are so pleasant on a spring afternoon.

At last Sir Albert's landau sweeps into view. He gets down and comes to me apologetically. He is a large, ruddy-faced bewhiskered man of pleasant disposition. This I can tell straight away. As to various other attributes and weaknesses he might or might not possess—time will be the telling. He instructs his driver, Eddington, to wheel my luggage cart to the landau. Eddington stands ramrod straight. His hands are large. I wonder as to his essentials. Large hands are the sign of a large cock, though I have found it not to always be the case. His big thumbs align perfectly with the side seam of his trousers as he bows to me. His face looks hewn from rock but his eyes are gentle. Perhaps I see in them a touch of the desire I so enjoy. The desire to humbly obey. He may make fine sport; we shall see. Sir Albert accompanies me to the carriage. As I extend him my gloved hand he kisses it. Then he helps me up. There is a knowing in his kiss, a worshipfulness.

The countryside is beautiful beyond compare. The road is pleasantly shaded and distant meadows bask in golden sunlight. Sir Albert asks if I mind his cigar. I do not and graciously allow him his pleasure, though he may well yet pay in some fashion for being late. How, I have not yet decided.

Sir Albert talks of Kenya. This bores me, although I pretend to listen politely and with interest. The road curves ahead. We pass over a stone bridge. The brook beneath is dappled and lovely. Its waters look shady and cool. Sir Albert interrupts his tales of Kenya to tell me that it flows through the grounds of Wellingham. We approach the estate. A fine brick wall surrounds the grounds. There is even an archway for the brook to enter. We pass through the gate. There are flower beds and lawns everywhere. The pruned hedges are impeccable. The house comes into view. A circular front between two extending wings. Servants await us on the steps. I am delighted. A summer of amusements is before me.

Sir Albert helps me down from the landau. The servants bow and curtsy. Two attract my eye. The first is the gardener, Totworth. He is a young man with golden hair. Even though it is worn short it is curly and thick. I would run my fingers through it but I restrain myself. I can see the muscles in his arms and chest through the thin material of his shirt. My eyes drop. His most important muscle bulges against the front of his trousers. The second is one of the upstairs maids. Her name is Clara. She is a pert, youthful little beauty with dark hair, green eyes and a slight sprinkling of freckles across her nose and cheeks. She returns my glance boldly, though without challenge. I sense in her a kindred spirit. I am informed that she has been selected by Sir Albert to be my maid. I know we shall get on famously.

The house is spacious and elegant beyond my hopes. The walls of the drawing rooms are satin above oak paneling. The library is vast and full of many leather bound volumes. I like the smell of it. I am shown up the wide, gently curving, carpeted staircase to my rooms. I have my own small drawing room and then my bedchamber. My windows overlook a small trellis-walled rose garden. I wonder if Totworth toils in it, and can readily imagine him toiling in my lush garden. Beyond is a small pavilion overlooking a pond created by a dammed-up brook. Flower beds are everywhere in the bright sunshine. I smile. I shall have no trouble mastering this household.

Far beyond the treetops past the flower beds on the far side of the pond I see the peaks of roofs. I am informed by Clara upon asking that it is the home of the Brigadier James Wimley and his young wife, Laura.

Clara assists me in dressing for dinner. Dinner is served in a finely appointed dining room. Sir Albert and I are alone at the huge table. I will change this. I love parties and company. Many things will have to change here at Wellingham. I can see that Sir Albert will be no obstacle to my designs. And as for the servants, they are but amusements.

I easily steer Sir Albert's mind along preset paths with my questions and comments. Sir Albert dearly loves London and would rather be there still, I think. He has no idea what a delight a home in the country well stocked with servants can be. We sip a fine claret. The servants move about in efficient silence.

That night Clara and I talk in my drawing room. She has a quick wit and is capable of much mischief, I conclude. I tell her that I need her assistance. She listens closely and with wide eyes. I am not one to delay the necessary workings of a plan. If I wish to control the house I must start with Sir Albert. Clara shall assist me. We shall begin tonight.

I carry a mild sleeping powder in a packet. I give some to Clara. I purchased it at a little chemist shop in Cologne. She will have no difficulty slipping a bit of it into Sir Albert's brandy. It will help him sleep, yet allow him to be partially wakened for a brief interval. The chemist in Cologne also told me it enhances romantic interest. How droll and dull a way to put it. I tell Clara it stiffens cocks, for that is truly what it does. She laughs. How audacious she is.

Late that night the household sleeps. Sir Albert sleeps better than most. But we shall soon wake him when the time is right. I furnish Clara with a black velvet mask and put one on myself. Clara helps me on with a tightly-laced black corset. My breasts spill over the front at the top. The nipples are visible and are dark cherries on the end of my mounds. My bottomcheeks thrust out exposed behind. Save for the brief corset, mask and black lace gloves, I am naked. My pussy is uncovered and is a pink smile in the dim light. Clara is wearing her maid's dress, cap and apron. If Sir Albert is able to see her in the dimness of his room he will not be able to tell which of the maids he sees, for the sleeping powder tends to fog the mind slightly. I don a robe for the trip down the long hall to Sir Albert's bedchamber. We move in silence. His door opens and shuts in silence behind us.

Sir Albert sleeps upon his back breathing heavily. The sleeping powder has taken effect. I drop my robe at the door. Clara and I tiptoe forward. Together we draw down the coverlet. His legs are spread with his bulging prick prominent under his nightshirt. I gently lift the garment and fold it back upon his belly. Clara is pleased with his attributes. I can see it in her eyes.

His balls are large and full. His penis, springing from a growth of hair on his belly, lolls thick and pendant. The head looks velvety-soft and inviting. I whisper soft instructions to Clara. She leans forward and grasps him in her palm. Gently she begins the working. The working of his foreskin. I move to the foot of his bed. I watch Clara's handiwork and stand ready. At the first sign of stirring I am prepared. He shall be enamored with me. I shall make him spill his seed in his dreams. Clara's hand is busy. It goads him to a fine erection. The shaft is thicker now, mapped with veins, and stands tall. The head is huge when the skin is drawn back. Would it were day. I would like to see the purple of it. The straining purple of the tip of his teased organ. Clara's hand is small on him. The huge penis is enslaved by the busy little hand moving up and down on his aroused member. Clara smiles. How she enjoys her handiwork. At last Sir Albert stirs.

I position myself. I face away from Sir Albert but look back over my shoulder to watch the frigging. I bend over and thrust out my bottom. When Sir Albert awakens he will see my straining globes. If it were day he would also see my pouting cunt surrounded by its halo of moss. My hair is up in a tight dark bun. I know the power of it. The tight proper bun and the bare bottom. The contrast will drive him mad. His eyes flutter open. He stirs and gasps. Clara lets go of him after several final forceful strokes. His cock looks as though it's going to burst. His eyes are on me now. I smile and wiggle my bare bottom. His hands grasp the sheet beneath him. He mumbles my name as a question. Then the spurting begins. His penis jumps and twitches. His sperm pours down the sides of his organ and soils his belly. It continues to ooze from the tip after the initial geyser subsides. It accumulates in a puddle in his deep navel and dribbles along his hips. His eyes are fevered, then dim as sleep retakes him.

Clara and I return to my rooms and collapse with laughter. How silly, yet how perfectly delightful. The wheels are turning now. He is in my hands and with him comes the household. Wellingham is mine. What games we shall play, Clara and I. Clara's face is flushed, as is my own. I would have amusements. I send her to Eddington's room on a matter of urgent business. Though it is late, they both return in but a few moments. Eddington stands waiting my instructions. No, I do not wish a carriage made ready. I wish to see Eddington's cock. The whip of my command descends upon his reservations. He complies. The maid and I watch him undress. His face is red. I stand before him still in corset and gloves and nothing else save the mask. Clara watches fascinated. She looks quite fetching in her black dress and frilly white apron and cap. Her cuffs are folded and starched. My cunt is exposed to Eddington's stare. He stands before us. He is hewn from marble. A great clublike organ hangs between his sturdy legs. His balls hang low, a sac full of big round plums.

I kneel upon the bed on all fours. "Clara, dear, lead him over by his prick, then jerk him to a full stand."

"As you say, Miss." Her hand grasps his thick tool, pulls him to me, and begins the motions. She pumps slowly, then faster and faster as he stiffens. His organ grows before my appreciative eyes. It lengthens and thickens; the helmet grows dark and enormous. His balls twitch as Clara continues running her clenched hand up and down. He gasps, trembles, then stands meekly. His eyes are wide. At last he is at full erection. I murmur my approval at the sight of him. Moisture oozes from the slit in his cockhead down over Clara's fingers. She has him drawn back. His foreskin is taut and red. How proper the dainty little maid looks even as she grasps the naked man's essentials. He is led closer. I tell Clara that I would like to have him licking at my quim. His balls become his leash in Clara's little hands. She instructs him well. He bends over obediently and I feel his tongue invade my lips. I love the feel of it. Clara has him tongue me from my slit to my anus. He is a feather that tickles me with a light sweeping motion back and forth across the bridge of flesh. Suddenly he lingers at my mount. Even Clara is surprised by his fervent tribute as he licks my mossy prominence. When he has thoroughly soaked the hair he ministers to the upper portion of each thigh, licking in long sweeps that end where my legs join my belly. Finally he descends on my pouting slit. I had intended that he should concentrate on my rearward orifice, but the sensations he elicits by lashing my pussybud weaken my resolve. He rolls my clit between his lips and then scrapes it with his teeth. His tongue is working at the fleshy folds and soon begins delving into my tunnel. He scours the sensitive membranes thoughtfully, sending excruciating jolts of pleasure through my body. Suddenly he withdraws his tongue; immediately I feel it at my anus. I soon come with delicious quiverings as his servile tongue thrusts in my circlet. I then have him back at my mount, wiping away my sprinkles with his lips and tongue.

I must reward Eddington for his valiant efforts. I shall reward Clara at the same time. I see the fever in her eyes. She wants to milk him and see him come. I have her sit on my dressing chair. Her lace apron is put in proper array upon her lap. I want to see him spill his seed on Clara's lap. I want her apron to receive his spurtings. I stand with hands on hips to view the spectacle. Clara takes his huge throbbing organ in her hands. She has technique. She does not grasp Eddington's penis at all. Rather she rolls it between the flats of both her hands. Eddington starts and his buttocks tremble. I feel my face flush at this sight of a huge organ in a milker's hands. The merciless little hands that shall not release it until it pours out its surrender.

I reach through from behind to grasp Eddington between the legs. His balls are heavy on my palm. He throws back his head and looks quite silly. Clara masturbates him and smiles. She runs her hand up and down his rigid shaft, frigging him with short, forceful jerks. Then she varies the motion so as to start his sperm boiling. She draws her palm all the way from his crown to the balls that I couch in my hand. Her fingers maintain their grip on his turgid flesh all the while, urging him to that delicious surrender. His cockhead is a purple mushroom that seems to expand even more before our eyes. The slit is open and gasping as Clara continues to pump him. I rub his balls at the same time, delighting in the way they roll about at the least pressure I exert. Eddington is so swollen now Clara is unable to close her fingers around his shaft. The veins stand out like a tracery of roads on a map. Suddenly his organ swells again and starts to twitch uncontrollably.

The spurting begins. Thick long strings of sperm spill down upon her starched apron. Eddington trembles mightily. I caress his balls and squeeze them gently in my gloved hand to aid the emptying. He sags weakly as the little hands coax the last bit of seed from him. Abruptly we tell him to dress. He is uncertain and confused as we calmly dismiss him. It is ever thus with males. They do not understand that once they are finished they are of no further use. How silly they are. How silly indeed.

The following morning Sir Albert is most gracious. His eyes are a bit haggard, however. There is longing in them. He longs for his dream to have been reality. He longs to spurt as I subtly wiggle my bare bottom and smile. I have deliberately worn my hair up. He has an eye for my tight bun. He spills a bit of food upon his coat at breakfast. I dab it up with my napkin and drift lightly across his cock with my fingertips, though I seem to take no notice. As I stand over him my breasts are in his face. "There, you're all clean now." There is fever in his eyes.

That afternoon Clara comes to me. One of the kitchen maids is with her, a young girl named Collette. Clara is angry. Collette is abashed. I am informed that there is a waist-high window between the kitchen and serving room. The cook's boy puts his organ through when he is unattended and has Collette suck it. She does not wish to, yet he is most insistent. He annoys her until she complies. I am furious. He shall lose his job, but will first be punished in another way. It will be a punishment we can all enjoy.

After soothing and calming Collette, Clara and I make our plans. The cook's boy expects Collette's services during the late afternoon when the kitchen is quiet. He is ready and waiting. He sees the black and white of a maid's uniform at the window at the appointed time. It is Clara. I am hidden in a pantry closet behind him. In my hand is a long birch rod. It has been soaking in water for several hours and is of the most exquisite suppleness. Collette said he would first expect her to handle him before the sucking. The cook's boy undoes his trousers and thrusts his organ through the aperture. Clara grips him. One hand is on the penis and one cups the balls.

She begins the motions. He gasps at the working of her hands. He stiffens readily. Then he asks for her mouth on him. Clara follows my instructions perfectly. She grasps his balls and tightens her fist. All the while her other hand continues the frigging. He tries to move her wrists in an effort to set himself free. She nearly unmans him. He cries out and realizes his helplessness.

I appear. Coolly I enquire, "What have we here? Have you no appointed tasks to perform that you spend the afternoon engaging in this lewdness?" A strangled gasp escapes him as he sees the birch. I raise it and begin the punishment. I adore the whistle of a birch rod through the air. I adore the slow striping of bare buttocks. His are pale and wide and will decorate nicely.

Clara's hands bind him well. He is quite defenseless.

His vulnerability amuses me. I take my time. I am an artist with the birch. A composer of symphonies. Symphonies of whistles, thwacks and moans. I bring the whip across one cheek, then the other. The lash hisses in the air as it descends. It leaves a red welt that slowly deepens in hue. I give him three parallel stripes on each buttock, then cross them with three more. As I do so I can feel the wetness growing between my thighs. This is truly a delightful way to pass the time! I decide to add a row of decorations across his upper thighs and lay to with all the strength in my arm. The birch descends and smacks with a sound that sends shivers through my pussy. Finally, after Clara confirms that the boy's organ is hugely erect—he is obviously enjoying his punishment as much as I am—I conclude the lesson with a pair of sweeping undercuts that catch him precisely between the buttocks and lick at his pendant balls. For the first time he howls unashamedly, though Clara tells me his tool has swollen even more. At last his bottom is well striped. I signal Collette. She has been waiting outside the door with the entire kitchen staff. They all enter and view the spectacle in stunned silence. I explain the punishment enough to give them all the fear of me. Proudly I show off my handiwork. The stripes on his bottom. They must wonder which upstairs maid has hold of him. Whose hands grip his sac and rub his male organ. She continues to pump, plying the turgid flesh with practiced fingers. She manipulates the balls with little twists and pinches. She has him at crisis now though he squirms and pleads. To spend before them all would be his ultimate horror of degradation. Clara makes his fears come true. After two long strokes she releases his penis and just maintains her purchase on his scrotum. She squeezes it so the spurting has only pain without the delight. He gasps and covers his face as his organ betrays him. His cock dances and flops about and he spills his seed down his legs and all over the sleeve of his tormentor. Clara releases him at last and he bends over groaning and cupping himself. I laugh at the stripes on his bottom. I laugh as he soils his own hands with his passionless flood in defense of his balls.

The servants fear me now. They are silly; they have nothing to fear as long as they are obedient. How amusing they are. That very afternoon the cook's boy is sent away. When I return to my rooms someone has filled a Waterford vase with fresh flowers. I smell them. I summon one of the maids to make me a nosegay. I would wear a fine nosegay at dinner tonight. I think of Sir Albert and his haunted eyes. I think tomorrow will be a fine day to tighten my fetters about him. Like a butterfly he shall be allowed his flutterings. But only within the confines of the glass case I shall slowly erect about him.The following day Sir Albert comes to me in the drawing room. I am perusing a small leather bound volume. It is a lecture on moral principles. I am bored. I pretend to be absorbed in my reading, however, and react with apparent hesitation when Sir Albert invites me to go on a carriage ride with him. At last I allow him to persuade me and I assent. There is pleading in his eyes. I am sure I will put an end to my boredom. A fine horse-drawn carriage is at the front. Eddington sits ramrod straight on the seat behind two splendid beasts. Sir Albert helps me up. I notice the calèche to be higher than the landau. The coaxing of a woman's hands in a man's lap would not be visible from this carriage.

The Oxfordshire countryside is beautiful. A carriage passes us near an ivy covered wall. Sir Albert nods. They are the Wimleys. I feel the man's eyes upon me as we pass. I have the pleasure of it. The pleasure of a man's eyes examining me, undressing me. Sir Albert is not himself. Minutes pass and suddenly he is kissing my hand and telling me I am beautiful. I laugh and tell him he is sweet. I say it is hot and put my feet up. I lift my skirts until my lace-stockinged legs are on display. My shoes have pointed toes with satin bows. I quite like the heels. I turn my ankles to admire my fine shoes. I am all in white. I lift my skirts higher and show him more, until he sees the garters that hold up the fine fabric caressing my thighs. Sir Albert gasps.

He unbuttons his trousers and draws out his huge cock. He really is quite desperate. His eyes are haggard, though apologetic. "For the love of God, please touch it Nina, I beg you."

I reach over. My hand draws back his foreskin and circles his shaft. "I'm sure this is very wicked. I shall certainly not make you spend." I work him a bit. He is swollen to bursting. I stare into his eyes, absorbing his expression of utter submission, while I run my hand up and down. I linger at the engorged cap, enveloping it, then resume stroking the hard pipe. I milk him until I feel the first twitch then snatch my hand away with an exclamation of disgust. He moans and the sperm spills from his thrumming tool all over his trousers and the seat. "Why must you make such a spectacle of yourself! Have you no decency?" He hangs his head in shame.

We return to the house. I snub Sir Albert for his lasciviousness. He is most penitent. Males are ever thus after they are drawn of their milk. When their penises are done spurting and their balls are empty their consciences return.

I need the solace of a tongue at my mount. A tongue clever in its prompting. A tongue to gently lick through the foliage of my cleft to find my center. I send Collette for Totworth. Collette is a conspirator now. She lacks Clara's natural propensities though I find her useful and most compliant.

Totworth appears before me. I order him to kneel. He has no place standing in my presence. First he must lick the satin bows of my shoes. His eyes question. Mine answer. He kneels. He is bashful in the licking at first. From my perspective I see only his blond curls and pink tongue. I have Collette disrobe him. My excitement builds as she tears the shirt from him. His chest and shoulders are broad. The muscles are like the breastplate of a Roman warrior I lick my lips as Collette takes the pants from him. He wears nothing underneath and turns to face me at my order. I am disappointed that his tool is but average. I will have him milked. It is delicious to have a male milked to softness while he nurses at one's cleft. In this way one is not annoyed with the rude erection. I have read of eunuches. I wish I could find one to lick me. It is more delightful when the tongue's humility is not prompted by the urgent balls, but rather by simple obedience. Collette begins milking him, then substitutes her mouth for her hand. Shameful! Yet I watch languidly. She lies beneath him as I raise my skirts. I am bare beneath. The lips of my quim pout for a licking, for the gentle quiet work of a servile tongue. I lean back in a great leather wing chair. Collette continues to take Totworth into her mouth, her throat, while he kneels at my feet and his tongue explores my slit. My pussylips swell from his gentle ministrations. I can see Collette licking him from stem to stern as he flicks at my pleasure-button. The tempo of his tongue coincides with the motion of Collette's head as she devours his throbbing tool. She takes his balls into her mouth now one at a time. Totworth groans and burrows deeply into my muff. His nose tickles me, but his tongue is doing far, far more. He licks and nibbles my clit as Collette more seriously mouth-fucks him. She swallows him again and again, moving her head up and down. He is gasping now. I can tell by the way his body begins to shake and spasm that he is flooding Collette's mouth with his sperm. Indeed, her cheeks are swollen and she gulps furiously. Meanwhile, Totworth's attentions are producing the desired effect. My body seems to be melting as I embark on a long, sensuous orgasm. I can feel the moisture run from my cleft down my thighs. His soft tongue intercepts the stream. I sigh and quiver until my skin is clean of my juices.

Later I sip tea out on the south lawn. I am bored. It is time I had guests. Guests to amuse me and with whom I can share my delights. I reminisce. Months ago when I was in Bavaria at the home of the Gräfin Von Echter we had many delights. The Gräfin was my mentor and Castle Schonring was my classroom.

I remember it vividly. The Gräfin and I sat in an elegant little drawing room. We had cakes and sherry. Her hair was the golden color of wheat. Her eyes were blue and her face was sweet with full pouting lips. She always wore her hair up. She was wearing a dress of black velvet brocade. A maid entered the room pushing a large four-wheeled cart with an oblong polished wooden box fastened to the top. It reminded me of a harp case I had once seen though it was shaped slightly differently. The cart was heavy but moved easily on oiled wheels. The Gräfin and I continued our conversation as the maid drew nearer. I could see that the cart was locked shut with three heavy padlocks. Beneath the cart resting on a shelf were a metal basin, two rolled towels and a small vial.

The maid wheeled the cart directly in front of the Gräfin. I was then quite startled to see a man's buttocks and genitals protruding through a small opening at one end of the cart. I realized that the man inside had to be on his back with his knees drawn up almost onto his chest. There was no other way that he could fit within the confines of the box. Whoever he was he was quite sealed in and helpless until someone should unfasten the locks and release him. My conversation with the Gräfin had ceased temporarily.

"Who is in the box?" I enquired. The Gräfin shrugged and raised her perfect eyebrows as if the identity of the prisoner was of no consequence whatever.

"One of the servants I should imagine."

She continued. "Nina, one of my delights is the manipulation of the male sexual organ. I find toying with such a thing to be relaxing and enjoyable and no hindrance to good feminine conversation. I daresay that I have with much practice become very proficient and I am certain that the individual in the box suffers a perfect excruciation of delight. Sometimes I allow the orgasm and sometimes I do not." I was quite shocked at these revelations. The Gräfin turned her attention to the maid. "Prepare him please, Erna."

The maid was a pretty pink-cheeked girl with knowing eyes. Her breasts swelled beneath her apron. She took the vial from the shelf of the cart and poured a little oil from it into her hands. She rubbed her hands together briskly for a moment then applied them to the genitals of the naked man in the box. I watched fascinated. While the maid rubbed and stroked the oil into the man's penis and balls the Gräfin continued her explanations.

"I have found myself wishing more than once that I could amuse myself with the male genital apparatus without having the accompanying male about to distract me with his moans, grunts, demands and pleadings. Hence the cart and box is a capital idea. The man is placed within some hours before I want to toy with him. In this way all his senses are quite deprived until the gentle fingering begins where he is most sensitive."

The maid finished her nimble fingering, leaving the poor wretch within the box very inflamed indeed. His penis, like the maid's hands, fairly glistened with the applied oil. The Gräfin dismissed the maid and then grasped the man's cock. She slowly began pulling his foreskin up and down. With her other hand she handled his sac. Within moments I realized that she was a consummate masturbatrix. I watched wide-eyed while she continued her manipulations. She directed the topic of our conversation back to French continental fashion.

As we talked of lace and elegant apparel she continued frigging the helpless male organ to a state of vast proportions. It was hugely swollen and from time to time she would gently draw the foreskin forward over the purple head. The Gräfin's hands became very moist indeed with the fluid of her prisoner's arousal. His cock was by now so large it seemed hardly able to contain itself or the geyser that threatened to erupt any second. It bobbed and twitched and fairly seemed to pulsate as the Gräfin continued to stroke it in a long, steady motion. We were talking of lace corsets when the poor wretch was too overwrought to contain himself any longer and spent. Thick heavy strings of sperm shot from him, liberally coating his tormentor's hands and wrists. She smiled and milked him dry, not even interrupting her train of thought for but a moment.

"Yes, Nina, I find that the finest corsets in all Europe may be purchased at a little shop in Rathmore Court in London."

Erna was summoned to wheel the spent victim of the Gräfin's handling away. I was stunned when she reappeared ten minutes later with another cart and a new victim. Erna wheeled the second cart to me and stopped. Once again she applied oil to her hands and worked it into the man's genitals, only this time the cart was at my chair. "I cannot," I sputtered. "I have never before done such a thing."

"Of course you can, Nina. One has but only to look at you to see that you have the knowing of it. It is in you, Nina, though latent, and I mean to bring it out full-fledged. I recognize myself in you. You were born to dominate and I will not see you fail your destiny."

My mouth went dry. I grasped the well-oiled penis before me and marveled at its velvet skin covering such hardness. It throbbed hotly in my hand. I closed my fist and began the milking.

"Don't neglect his balls. The good milker always handles the balls."

Was it gasping I heard from within the wooden box? I played the milkmaid until the spurting began. As the sperm drenched my hands my eyes met those of the Gräfin. My cheeks were flushed, for I had spent as well.

CHAPTER II

Some days later Sir Albert's nephew and his new wife, Nannette, arrive. We meet them at the entry. Percival Archibald James Wellingham is a fop. Sir Albert has quite a ridiculous nephew. He kisses my hand and tries to look the gallant. He says something about a young woman of fair beauty. I laugh. I cannot restrain it. I laugh in his face. His wife looks at me. I can see it all. She is his better, yet treated as his inferior. How often it happens that the woman of superior intellect finds she must be the obedient wife of an idiot and must hang on his every word. I will see to it that things change.

My chance comes the following day. I have a lounge chair set up for me in the trellised flower garden. I sit and read a volume of poetry. In the warm sunshine I slip off my shoes. My silk stockings are the most fine available and of white lace. I have my feet up before me. I have been told many times that they are well shaped, but that they are a faint hint of the splendor of my thighs.

I read and daydream in the sun. Suddenly I hear Clara's voice from the other side of the rose hedge. "Miss, please do not let on, but Sir Albert's nephew is nearby peering at you through a break in the hedge. I fear he is stimulating himself. He has his prick out and he is rubbing it."

I pretend to stifle a yawn and with my hand concealing my mouth I instruct Clara. "When he spends raise a shout and I will come running. Then he will be our plaything for fear of a shameful scandal." Clara hastens back to her vantage point ready to do my bidding at the proper time. I consider what specifically must have aroused his ardor. I can only conclude that the sight of a pretty young woman's stockinged feet and legs must arouse the lust in him. I smile and pretend to read on in my flowery volume of love poetry. With one hand I reach down and draw up my skirts a bit as if in enjoyment of the warm sunshine.

I raise one foot above the other as if stretching, thus giving him a view quite up above my thighs. I know my pussy, bare and faintly visible beneath my upraised garment, is exposed to his gaze. I sigh and smile apparently at something I am reading. I wiggle my toes. Slowly I let one hand drift down to my belly, then lower still to my thighs. Almost absentmindedly I let my fingers raise my skirt impossibly high. They linger on the curvaceous expanses of flesh and begin to move toward my mount. I can just imagine Percy's eyes; they must be starting from his head by now! My pussy is now fully exposed to the warm rays of the sun—and to Percy's gaze. I run my fingers through the silken thatch that adorns it and massage the outer folds. Suddenly I close my eyes, stretch languidly, and drive two fingers directly into my slit! They penetrate up to the knuckles. I hear a faint intake of breath then a shrill outcry from Clara. "Oh, Miss, come quick! What a debauchery! What lewdness!" I lower my skirt, slip on my shoes and hasten around the corner to the spot. Percy is trapped between Clara and me. He has his cock tucked back into his trousers and is desperately fumbling with his shirt. His jacket is all askew. Shining thick white stains are on his clothes, the grass and the rose leaves. I note with satisfaction that he has paid a rather generous tribute to my feminine charms. Clara and I close in.

"Percy, dear, don't tuck it away just yet," I laugh. Clara grasps his arms and holds them behind him. He does not struggle. I stroke his cheek. He is trembling with shame and quite speechless. I laugh again. What a curiosity he is.

I brazenly take down his trousers and drawers. His legs are shaking. His tool is softening though still inflamed and very wet. I take it daintily between my thumb and forefinger. It is still moist from the ejaculation. I decide to play games with him.

"What were you doing behind the hedge, Percy? I trust you were not engaging in an act of which you would not want Nannette to find out. Such a revelation could be the ruin of you."

"Please, Nina, I would be most grateful for your kind silence," he manages to stammer while his cock stiffens between my fingers. I gently torment it with deft half-strokes.

"Of course you shall. You shall have my silence for a

time and for a price." I pump him to full hardness then wipe my hand on his shirt. "Percy, I expect complete obedience from you. You will not speak unless addressed. Clara, be a dear and help him off with all his clothing as soon as he lays down on his back on the grass."

With Clara's assistance he is compelled to lay down and divested of all his clothing. We are gentle. I want him to tongue me. Today it is not my cleft that craves the attention, but my ass. I decide to do what I have seen the Gräfin demonstrate more than once. I shall "queen" Percy. I raise my dress. He already knows that but for my stockings I am naked beneath. I stand over him facing his feet. I then squat down bringing my bare bottom firmly down onto his face.

Clara takes him by the balls to assure his compliance with my every whim. His labored gasping for air warms my bottom and I successfully quell the urge to laugh at the sensation. Clara squeezes his essentials. She orders him to begin the licking. I reach up and straighten my hat. The woman must be dignified in her enjoyment of the servile male tongue. His tongue gently licks at my anus. Then softly probes within. Yes, this is most definitely great fun. And while it provides me with a delicious serving of pleasure, it also reinforces to the male his abject surrender and the extent of the degradation to which he is willing to descend. Percy is the quintessential case in point as he laps at my bum and licks the taut ring of muscle at its center. He scours me thoroughly while I press my bottom down upon him. His organ swells. Clara grasps it now and gently strokes it. The skin is drawn back from his head and it looks quite ready to burst. Poor Percy is such a boor but he has a willing and trainable tongue. He tongues me with more force now and fairly thrusts it into my fundament. I begin to come in great roiling waves that originate deep in my belly. My sprinkles copiously moisten his chin.

"I fear he is going to spend, Miss." I heed Clara's warning and reach down to sharply pinch Percy at the base of his root. His spasm subsides, though mine continue. Minutes pass slowly with delicious multiple orgasms.

Finally we get up. I straighten my skirts and hat. We look down at him and laugh at the sight of his stiff, forlorn prick.

"I may perhaps need your services again. At least there is something for which you have a little talent, Percy." With this I extend my foot and nudge his swollen organ with my shoe. With a moan of shame he comes. It is thick and slowly slides down the sides of his shaft to trickle onto his balls. We leave him.

Later that afternoon Nannette and I at last have a private talk. We converse about varied subjects and exchange sundry anecdotes. With gentle steering and much aplomb I bring our topic to rest upon the relationship between the sexes. Collette pours us tea from a finely-wrought silver service. "I sometimes find myself entertaining the notion that men are the weaker sex. They are so easily led and so very basic and predictable in their tastes and passions."

"How so? I am not certain I fully understand your meaning," Nannette enquires.

"One has only to objectively view a man's pursuits. They are all either in some way related to the procurement of food, drink, or the sexual act. So much of what they do and say is simply geared to the establishment of what is called in dealing with animals or primitives—a pecking order. If their bellies are full and they are, pardon the expression, *titillated* sensually, they are quite content. All their ambitions and drives center about these basic needs. Hardly more of a goal than a wild animal has to aspire to. Conversely women are far more spirited. They easily come to relish power for the sake of power alone and indeed have often wielded such behind the scenes. I daresay that women perhaps control much already and suffer the male figureheads only because they are needed to cope with the more tedious and day to day aspects of authority. The female has too much imagination to allow herself to be compromised by such a draining regimen. Oh, Nannette, I fear I am not a gracious hostess. Will you have more tea?"

Nannette accepts my offer and listens to my continuing

discourse with fascination. I can see my words are hitting the mark. I shall make of her what she has always been destined to be. A woman fully aware that the world is at her feet.

"Truly, Nannette, have you never wondered why it is men suffer themselves to be led to war. Women would disdain such submission. It is men who toil in mines, mills and fields."

"Nina, you amaze me. Some ideas of this sort have crossed my mind from time to time but you have assembled them with perfect clarity."

I beg Nannette's pardon and continue on a slightly more explicit vein. "Even when it comes to the sexual parts, Nannette, even here the natural superiority of the woman is obvious. The male hangs vulnerable and exposed while the woman is internalized like a closed blossom containing great promise. After the coital act itself men are spent and drained of their strength while women frequently have just begun. One might say that the rutting bull too soon expires." Our conversation continues and after many exchanges I interject, "The private parts of the male are so suited to a woman's dominion. The penis hangs exposed so easy for the feminine hand to cajole. And the balls so sensitive to touch make an excellent bridle of control. When a lady has a man's essentials in her hand both fully realize the truth of their separate stations."

Nannette flushes crimson at my words but listens with rapt attention. Our talk continues and we find much in common. Soon we are laughing together like old friends. It is at this point that I choose to break some rather disturbing news to my new confidant. With hushed voice and apologies I tell her of Percy's lewd indulgence in the garden. I omit the queening episode, however, deeming the time not ripe for full divulgence. I offer a sympathetic shoulder and state my support through Nannette's resulting outburst of tears. I apologize lest I should have unwittingly in some way provoked his lasciviousness. She assures me that I am blameless. I offer suggestions of possible retributions. They are accepted. Together we conspire delights of vengeance.

A day after my talk with Nannette, Sir Albert takes ill. In some obscure way I believe he fancies himself in love with me. It is rather pathetic really. He stays in his room and refuses to eat. He pouts. He thinks himself ill, yet his curing would be absurdly simple. He longs for my hand on his sex organ. He longs for me to masturbate him. Since the incident in the carriage I have spurned him and this he cannot seem to bear.

Evening falls; I plot with Nannette. We shall have amusements with Sir Albert tonight. At the evening meal we have Percy between us. I realize the long lace tablecloth can hide my fingering. While Percy talks pompously of parliamentary intrigue, I place my hand in his lap. I undo his trouser buttons one by one. I reach in and pull out his sleeping tool. Gently, yet insistently, I pump it to throbbing wakefulness. His pompous talk dies out and beads of perspiration break out on his brow. I work him steadily, just moving my hand and wrist so no upper arm movement will reveal me. Nannette is still very angry with him. She and I talk together of gardening and the proper planting of floral patterns. We ignore poor Percival. He is ignored by all but my hand. He is driven to distraction. What an amusement it is to milk a male in a public place.

The helplessness of males becomes them I think. Percy holds his fork tightly. His knuckles are white. I ask him to hand me the sauce. His hand shakes so much that he almost drops it on the tablecloth. I turn from him and converse with Nannette even as I feel his twitchings begin. I then grasp him more tightly and draw his velvet sheath of skin down hard and hold him so. He has a helpless strangled look as the spurting begins. His penis spasms in my hand and I feel the hot thickness of his sperm spill over my wrist. I wipe my hand on his trousers and use his own napkin for the rest.

He excuses himself and leaves the room, almost bumping Collette who is entering with the dessert tray. She stares at the stains on his front and gives him a mocking smile. The Gräfin once told me that the male is enslaved by the milking of his cock. The pleasure is severe and poignant. They are soon hopelessly addicted to the skill of the female hand. The hand that drains them of their strength.

After dinner Nannette and I go up to my rooms. Percy reads forlornly alone in a downstairs drawing room. Upstairs Clara assists us. Nannette and I shall see to Sir Albert's needs. Nannette is naked save for crisp lace gloves. They are starched to perfection. Sir Albert shall feel maximum friction when she is his milker. The thatch at her mount is dark and full. I would like to see a male nursing there. Her breasts are large and her nipples are pointed and wide enough to satiate a regiment. I also am naked and Clara helps me place my hair up in a bun. Sir Albert will again be maddened by the contrast between my severe bun and bare bottom. I have the taste for it. Nannette compliments my fulsome buttocks. They are firm and round and quite defy gravity, she says. We laugh. I have Clara bring me the wide-brimmed short-crowned Spanish hat I purchased in Segovia. Save for it I shall be naked. Clara angles it so it is down in my eyes in front and up in back. It sets off my tight bun deliciously. I am pleased with what I see in the mirror. We don robes only for the passage down the hall to Sir Albert's room. We slip within and doff our coverings. Clara stands outside the door to keep all others out. Once again I kneel at the foot of his bed. My bottom is toward him. Nannette draws down his covers and lifts his nightshirt. She turns it back upon his chest. His cock is massive even in repose. Her eyes sparkle at the sight of him.

Nannette awakens him by stroking his brow with her lace-gloved hand. He moans, starts and awakens. His eyes are startled. They dart from me to Nannette. My bottom rests on my bare heels. I smile at him and Nannette begins the stroking. The organ swells quickly and becomes fat with arousal. How indecent it is. A woman's gloved hand gently enslaving a naked male organ. She pumps him heartily, up and down, giving his engorged shaft a subtle twist every so often to vary the motion of the masturbation. She sucks him when her inexperienced arm becomes fatigued. I did not think she would willingly take a male organ into her mouth, but she swallows Sir

Albert's without the least hesitation. His eyes are wide and glazed as her head bobs. His tool glistens as she tongues the length of his shaft. The swollen head pops from her mouth like a confection. She tongues it all around and sweeps across the gasping slit. Then she gobbles the entire shaft to the balls once more and begins massaging it with her hand on the upstroke. Suddenly Sir Albert is raising his bottom off the bed. He cries out and comes thickly. As he is drained his fevered eyes are fixed on my bottom. I wiggle my hips as I watch the spurting. I would have prolonged it before his first spending. But I could see Nannette's mouth was most persuasive. She would bob her head and tighten her lips in the working of his organ. A motion that he found most undeniable.

"Dear Sir Albert, you must indeed be feeling less constrained."

Nannette laughs at my utterance. She rolls his sperm between her gloved fingertips. I move back and stand over him smiling. Then I sit full upon his face. His whiskers tickle my cleft.

"There is medicine for your illness in my cleft. Gently draw it out with your tongue." He obeys with alacrity. His tongue first dabbles then explores my depths. There is famishment in the work of his tongue. He withdraws his tongue after a bit and nurses at my clit like a hungry child. He worries the little nub of flesh between his teeth, being careful not to exert too much pressure…for he knows the price I will exact should that happen. He is a humble and appreciative enough lapdog. He strokes my sensitive flesh with his tongue and delves into my delicious tunnel after thoroughly laving my mount and cunt lips. He flicks at the pink inner membranes and plays them like the strings of a harp. Delicious tingles spread all through my belly and I release the flood of my passion. His tongue sounds the depths of my cleft again. I mew and wiggle myself upon him. I bite my lip, my cheeks feel like hot coals. Nannette is at him again with her gloved fingers. The crisp lace is rubbing him nearly raw. I watch her work him as he licks me. Again she makes him come. I have a full feast of pleasure there upon Sir Albert's face. Yet again Nannette works his swollen tool. Her hands coax and demand more tribute from his balls. His shaft rises in response, though not nearly so quickly. As he gently bites my nub and I spend again he is forced to orgasm. Barely anything comes from his organ, though it twitches for a long while in Nannette's gloved fist. His balls are empty.

We have drained him. He is spent and useless. I get up off him and he kisses my hand over and over again and thanks me. Nannette pulls off her soggy gloves and he kisses her hands as well. We leave him. We leave him drained and lying in a thick puddle of his own sperm.

Back in my rooms Nannette is unfulfilled. The lips of her quim pout for a licking. We have Clara bring Eddington. He is relieved of his clothing and we have him lie on his back on the carpet. Nannette's eyes are on his huge penis. She wants him to fuck her. Instead I have her sit upon his face. I instruct him to tongue her bottom. I am his teacher and am most explicit in my demands. I have him hold his tongue out as stiff as it can be. Then Nannette wiggles her bare bottom against his standing tongue. His wet little prodder penetrates her like a penis until his lips are glued to the crack between her buttocks. He roves around inside her, stroking, licking, while her eyes roll and the color rises in her face. He is reaming her well, I can see, and I am almost disappointed I did not claim the pleasure for myself. Yet I like to be generous, particularly when the servility of the male is involved, and I take satisfaction in the way Eddington sucks Nannette's ass. I can tell he is darting the tip of his tongue into her now the way he would his cock if I permitted it. Nannette is almost overcome by the sensations that emanate from her bottom. She gasps and spends. I watch her nipples harden with amusement. I relent and tell Eddington he may now bury his prick in Nannette's ready cunt. He needs no prompting. Nannette turns on her back and spreads her legs wide. Her pussy is already slippery from the enormity of her previous spending. Beads of moisture glisten on her thatch as Eddington moves between her thighs. His cock is enormous and like a dowsing rod points straight at her slit. I sit back to better enjoy what will follow. The huge cockhead prods Nannette's taut lips and with a single thrust is wedged inside them. Nannette gasps and her eyes fairly bug from her head. With short strokes Eddington begins to bury his length in her eager receptacle.

"Come on now," I encourage him. "The lady is waiting for you to perform as she expects you to. And if you fail to give satisfaction," I warn, "there will be dire consequences." I stand and give him a hearty slap on the buttocks that drives his cock more deeply into Nannette's cunt.

This is all he needs. He rears back and rams his lance fully in to the balls. Nannette cries out and locks her legs around his back. She sees nothing and hears nothing, only feels that humongous pole plumbing her depths.

Eddington is anxious to please. He fucks her with long, steady strokes that have Nannette murmuring with delight. This is how it should be, I reflect. The servile male pleasuring his mistress upon command. Unfortunately, the male tires so quickly and is usually useless after a single episode.

I reach under to feel Eddington's balls as he drives in and out of Nannette's pussysheath. They flop against her upturned buttocks with each forceful stroke. He drills her well, varying his motion from time to time, rotating his hips so as to stretch her slit, and altering the position of her legs so as to affect the depth and angle of penetration of his cock.

Nannette squirms in delight and a warm glow begins to suffuse her body. She moans quietly and tells Eddington to fuck her harder. He does, fairly jamming his prick into her stuffed pussy. Three more strokes and I can feel his balls begin to pulse. Nannette is spending as I pull Eddington off her. His cock twitches and jumps and a geyser of thick sperm shoots from the tip to land on Nannette's belly and thighs. I pump his shaft hard and milk every last drop from him as Nannette stretches luxuriously on the carpet in the afterglow of her orgasm.

Afterward Nannette and I decide that Percy shall have his comeuppance the following day. It dawns bright, warm and fair. Nannette and I ask Percy to take a carriage ride with us in the closed coupe. He is most flattered and believes that he has been forgiven. How little he knows. How absurd he is. We chatter and laugh as the carriage takes us about on the nearby roadways. We have Eddington stop at a small copse of trees. There is questioning in Percy's eyes. Eddington remains with the coupe while Percy accompanies us into the wood. We stop beneath a chestnut tree in a small clearing. Nearby a bee hums and a butterfly sails lazily through the flowers.

"Percy, I fear we shall have to punish you for the obscenity in the rose garden. Take off all your clothes please, and do so at once." My voice stings him like a martinet and he obeys. Soon he stands before us naked, his cock limp and wrinkled with his clothes in pathetic disarray on the grass.

Nannette addresses him next. "Percival, I am ashamed of you. I cannot find words to adequately convey to you the extent of my disgust and anger. Obey our every command now and submit to what is in store, or what you will receive otherwise shall make this appear as a kindness." He hangs his head. Poor, dear Percy is so easy to despise. Nannette tells him to lean against the chestnut tree with his bottom out and his palms upon its trunk. His penis hangs, though it is slowly thickening. It is in complete submission to the female that the erotic potential of the male is fully realized. Any young governess would state the truth of this. A young governess who sees her charge naked from the waist down and hotly erect before his caning.

I find a small birch thicket and break from it a stout supple limb. I would have it soaked in brine first, however its condition cannot be helped. I stand behind Percy and begin his birching. There is something delightful in the long, slow whipping of a naked man by fully-dressed women. It is leisurely and most gratifying. I lay dozens of stripes on his bottom until it looks quite ready to burst into flame. Then Nannette applies the rod. She makes it dance upon the backs of his thighs until he is quite insane with the pain of the moment. His pleadings and whimperings do not suffice to halt or ease his torment. She lays it on furiously, carefully birching across the cheeks. Then she administers a vicious undercut that licks him between the thighs and nips his balls. It tears a pathetic scream from his throat, though his cock is fully erect.

Finally his ordeal is ended. We stand beside him then and make him rub himself to spending. He does not want to do such a thing in front of his smiling tormentors. Yet, in his agonized state he is most pliable and at last complies. We watch him work his own organ. He has a fine hard-on. The head of his piston is swollen to great dimensions and his plums swing at the motion of his fist. We have him milking himself still leaning against the tree with his bottom out and his legs spread. One hand supports him. His eyes are closed and his breath comes quickly. He has done this before, for his practiced motion brings him to the brink of orgasm. We laugh as his spurtings drench the grass. Then we take the coupe back to Wellingham and leave him to find his own way back. He is naked, for we have taken his clothes.

That evening Nannette and I sip a fine old Port and converse. Poor Percy has slunk back scarcely an hour ago. He has retired to his room much shaken and humbled. For an amusement we have Sir Albert wait on us. He is most humble and would have been well served by a lower social standing. I tell Nannette of the Gräfin and how excellent a finishing school for young ladies Schonring castle was.

"Nannette. I well remember one afternoon as if it were yesterday. Beyond the main castle courtyard and through a small postern gate was an enclosed outer yard. Within this yard was a stable, though it was like no stable that you have ever seen or heard of, I am sure. Erna came up to my chamber and bade me follow her downstairs. She told me that the Gräfin had in mind some further teaching for me that very day. When we gained the bottom of the steps I was most surprised to see the Gräfin playing the milkmaid. She wore a black dress which came barely below her knees. It was embroidered in the front with red and yellow branches and flowers. Beneath this sleeveless high-collared dress she wore a fine, full-sleeved snow-white blouse. Her golden hair was woven into two long thick braids that came full down to her tiny waist. Her feet were bare. She looked young and beautiful. She certainly looked much younger than her thirty-five years though she carried herself with an assuredness that only maturity can grant."

"She must be a truly rare beauty indeed," Nannette breaths.

"Oh yes, Nannette, she is. Well, as I was saying, there she stood. She told me to change into similar apparel. When I finished and stood before her clad as she was, she smiled at me and told me that I looked quite fetching. I then followed her through the main courtyard and beneath the postern into the side yard where stood the stable. We entered and I found myself in an outer room. Four shallow wooden buckets had been placed on the hay-strewn floor.

"The Gräfin told me that I should act with dignity and reserve when we passed inside the main room of the stable. She said that I should play the part of a peasant milkmaid and not let the cattle within distract me in any way. She told me to watch her for a bit and then follow her example.

"She opened a small oak cupboard in the corner of the stable's outer chamber and withdrew two three-legged milking stools. Thus, following her holding two buckets with my left hand and my milking stool with my right, I passed into the stable. Oh, Nannette, you shall not believe your ears when I tell you this. What a sight!

"There, before us, suspended from the ceiling on metal rods, were two rows of cattle stanchions stretching away into the dimness. However, they were not quite cattle stanchions as they were too small for the necks of four-legged cattle. Though they were just the proper size for what they did contain."

Nannette is wide eyed. "Oh, Nina, you are cruel. Don't drag it out so. Tell me what form of cattle were there."

I can tell by her flushed face that she suspects the truth already. "They were men, Nannette. Naked males and they were upon all fours like beasts." Nannette gasps and shudders with delight. She urges me on with my tale. Sir Albert's hand shakes as he fills our glasses again from his private stock. His hand shakes not from the casual wasting of the priceless port, but rather from the effect of my tale. He is quite stricken. I continue. "The Gräfin was quite business-like, really. She went to the first male in the line and set down her stool by him. She sat down upon it and placed a wooden bucket beneath the male's huge cock. Then without more ado, she grasped his weapon and began milking him. I watched in astonishment. I had thought the wretch already erect before she started, his prick was of such vast proportion. But it was not so.

"He stiffened even more until his tool hung hoselike with the tip almost brushing the bottom of her bucket. I can tell you, Nannette, that the sight of her perfect hands masturbating that great tool made my quim itch in a most maddening way. As she worked him he shook his head, causing the stanchion to clang against its supporting rod. He was just like a great animal, but the hands of his milker were suave in their demands. As the Gräfin continued the milking other males in the stable stirred and became aroused. My eyes fairly danced from the sight of one huge penis to the other. They all stiffened, for they knew what was going to be done to them. They knew they were going to be drawn of their sperm and find release in a milkmaid's goading hands.

"I stood behind the male that the Gräfin was milking to watch his huge plums swing. His sac hung so low, Nannette, that I fairly tingled."

Sir Albert's breeches are all tented in front. The nuances of my story are not lost on him. Nor are they lost on Nannette. She calls Sir Albert to her and undoes his trouser buttons. His cock springs free, erect and glistening at the tip. Then she begins to manipulate his rigid tool. It fairly throbs and steams in her dainty grasp. I must admit I am pleased at the effects of my tale. I proceed.

"At last, the Gräfin's hands had him at crisis. He threw back his head and with a strangled grunt he came. Hot, thick strings of sperm splashed into the wooden bucket followed by more as he was pumped dry. The Gräfin's hands were greased with his spendings.

"At last, when he had fully ejaculated and sagged forward in his exhaustion, the Gräfin looked over her shoulder at me. She said, 'Nina, the other side is yours. Perhaps you had better begin, for you have much to do.' I turned in obedience to her instruction. 'Oh, Nina, milk all but Number Five. Handle him, but do not let him orgasm. I shall not allow him to come for a fortnight. His organ is the biggest and I am saving his sperm for later amusements.'

"Beneath my skirts the lips of my cunt fairly pouted when I took the first huge male organ in my hand. My breasts rose and fell and I could feel my nipples harden beneath my blouse. I sat down upon my stool and arched my bare feet against its legs. As I reached beneath my victim to grasp his cock I shook my hair out of my eyes and looked up to see a placard fixed above his stall. I was at number one. The Gräfin was milking the even-numbered side and I was milking the odd-numbered side. The huge penis would be the third one I was to handle."

Nannette's hand drives Sir Albert to distraction. His prick is swollen. She has drawn his cock out from the gap in his trousers and they hang at his trouser front, fat and indecent. Nannette recognizes the signs of impending orgasm and releases his tool for a time. Sir Albert's face is flushed and his lower lip trembles.

My story unfolds. "I made the first male give up his sperm in just a few moments. I jerked him hard and I fear, a bit harshly in my inexperience. Yet, he did not seem to notice. His juice was thick and hot upon my fingers. In my enthusiasm and inexperience I was rather slovenly. As much of his milk fell upon the hay as fell into the bucket. When I moved to the next male I was more careful and prolonged his handling. When at last my working fist gave his swollen shaft and balls relief his thighs knotted and tensed in time to the twitches of his cock in my grasp. At the risk of being thought to have no decorum, I must tell you that my cunt was quite wet. I could feel my swollen clit bringing me near to spending. I moved my stool and bucket to the next station. There knelt the male of truly vast proportion. My eyes glazed at the sight of his genitals. I grasped him. It took both my hands to circle his vast girth. I commenced his teasing. I pumped him ever-so-gently. When his organ began to throb and jerk and seemed near spending, I would release it for a bit and gently bounce his sac upon my open palm. Then, as I grasped and kneaded his balls I quivered and came in a rush."

Nannette begins with Sir Albert's penis again. She urges me on with my tale.

"I handled him for a very long time. I could not resist it. I toyed with his balls and masturbated him. I rubbed his organ against the underside of his belly with the flat of my hand. I worked his foreskin to and fro so much that he was of such hardness I could no longer draw it over the head again. At last I released him and went on to the next. Number Five bit his lip and trembled in an agony of longing as my hands left him. But the Gräfin had trained him well. He made not a sound, though his pleading eyes spoke volumes. I could see old scars on his buttocks from the dancing of the Gräfin's whip. I went on to the next."

Nannette has Sir Albert at crisis. Her glass is empty, drained of all its port. She holds it beneath his swollen cockhead and fists him gently. I lean forward to watch the spurting. I want to see the slit in his tip disgorge a torrent of sperm. It does not disappoint me. He spurts into the glass Nannette holds. A fine old vintage of thick manhood. We send him away. Nannette questions me.

"So when was the male with the hugest prick of all finally milked of his seed?"

"A fortnight later the Gräfin had a ball. One of her guests was a noblewoman from a country whose name I forget. The Gräfin brought the poor fellow in with a post over his shoulders to which his wrists were fastened. The noblewoman was then permitted to milk him into a bottle in front of all the guests. He was most copious. Of course he was not used solely for that purpose. Once he had been wrung dry of the load of sperm that had been stored in his balls for so long, he was made to fuck the noblewoman in front of the assembled multitude. It was quite a sight. A couch was dragged to the center of the room. The male, after being freed of his bonds, was told to lie upon it. His hands were rebound above his head and fastened to the arm of the couch. His cock, still engorged even after having been emptied, stood straight out from his belly. It was so huge I do believe we could have flown a flag from it.

"It took some doing for the Gräfin to convince the noblewoman to take him there in front of us, for she was ashamed to expose herself naked. Finally, though, the sight of that amazing pole convinced her. She disappeared from the room for several minutes and reappeared wearing a cape that covered her completely from shoulders to ankles. When she reached the couch she dropped the garment and stood revealed in a corset that left exposed everything below her shapely hips. Her mount was liberally tufted with hair and her slit was wide and pink. She moved immediately over the erect cock and had to stand upon the couch because of its length. She reached down and took it in her hands and stroked it while she lowered herself until the thick head was against her cunt. Then she slowly descended. Her mouth hung open as that immense helmet became wedged inside her slit. I thought the thing would split her, but her opening stretched and stretched and finally accepted it. She hesitated a moment there, gasping for breath, then continued apace. She lowered herself onto the mast, commenting all the while how she could feel it in her belly, how it was tearing her apart, how it threatened to emerge from her mouth. Yet she never wavered and finally dropped completely upon the shaft. When it was completely inside her she smiled and began to rock back and forth, thrusting her hips in a milking motion that would soon wring an additional load of sperm from her prisoner. She continued her steady rhythm, then raised herself up slowly and squatted. In that position she began impaling herself again and again in short jumps. It was most impressive seeing that incredible staff appearing and disappearing as she fucked herself to her satisfaction. The Gräfin urged her on as did all the guests, clapping and shouting encouragement. We all drew closer as the woman's breath began to come in short gasps that heralded the onset of her orgasm. The poor fellow beneath her lay docilely while she milked him, though the set of his jaw and a quivering of his lips showed he, too, was near the brink. Finally he exploded in her, drenching her cavern with a flood of sperm that spilled past her stuffed pussylips and dribbled back onto his own thighs. As for the noblewoman, she was bucking and moaning her pleasure and came at much the same moment as her captive, I think. She was so drained by her excruciatingly ecstatic ordeal that we had to assist her off the slowly diminishing cock buried in her pussy."

Nannette laughed and asked of the Gräfin's origins.

"All I am certain of is that she is of nobility also. In the war with the French, Schonring was used as a prison for captured French officers. It was rumored that she interrogated them herself while they were strapped down naked. She would have been just eighteen at the time. It is said that she had them telling all. None could withstand her."

Two days pass. I feel it is high time Totworth is seen again. So I summon Clara and Collette. I ask them to bring Totworth to my room. I am in need of satiation by a male tongue. I say they must bring him to me naked. Collette flushes, but Clara smirks. How different they are. How they compliment each other.

They soon return. Totworth is naked between them. Clara has hold of his prick. She tells me that she led him up the stairs by it and down the hall. I compliment her and tell her she is inventive. She must also be circumspect. Totworth's cock is very swollen from Clara's fingerings. She is fortunate by the look of him that his spendings did not soil the hall carpet. Though his size is average only, his shaft and balls are so pink and smooth they can be captivating and lure the female hand.

I want him to fuck Clara while he tongues me. I slip on white gloves and make him stand at attention. His penis quivers. I play the military officer. I subject Totworth to a long and most detailed white glove inspection. I am most thorough. I examine the thick red helmet, then lift the shaft so as to get a better view of his pendant balls. Clara and Collette are amused as they watch. I inspect Totworth until he almost spurts in my hand.

I am naked beneath my dress. Undergarments are such an inconvenience in fine weather. I kneel on the window seat, raise my dress and rest my arms on the sill. Collette brings Totworth forward. She holds him by his balls and has him kneel at my bottom. I want him at my bum. I so command him. My ass only today. His tongue swirls about it in gentle tentative lickings. Then he licks over the ring of hard muscle of my anus. I am hot; I feel the heat of the licking in my legs and belly. My nipples harden into my arms. He thrusts his tongue into my fundament. Meanwhile, Clara has crawled beneath him after having removed her clothes. Her nakedness is an invitation. Her skin is so smooth; her breasts are wide and slightly flattened as she lies on her back beneath the man who licks my ass. She spreads her legs and guides his rampant cock to her creamy, lightly-mossed slit. He is surprised, but he responds eagerly as he continues to probe my tunnel. With a single thrust of his hips he drives his tool into Clara's grasping box. I can tell he penetrates her deeply because his tongue is suddenly well within my bumhole. He fucks me with his tongue, totally subservient and eager to please, as he fucks Clara with his prick. He pushes into me with steady strokes as his shaft explores Clara's passage. She murmurs that she is pleased with his skill and his desire to pleasure her. She thrusts her hips back up against him to draw his cock more deeply into her. She falls over the precipice almost immediately and spends. Before he can match her, however, she pushes him away. I silently applaud her presence of mind. She truly knows the proper way to instruct males in the intricacies of servitude.

Totworth is disappointed, but I draw his attention back to his task at my bottomhole.

I tell him not to stop. Again his tongue probes my butthole. He has the way of it. His tongue knows the way of a pretty woman's bottom. He can see my buttocks before him. My back is arched. I have pulled my dress up above my hips. He penetrates my anus with his tongue. I tense ever so slightly and gently force him out. He stiffens his tongue and again craves entry. I relax my muscles and he tongues me deeply. I come once again in a delicious wave. My parts are aflame with the delight of it. I look at my hands as the pleasure subsides. My sapphire ring catches the sunlight of the window. The Gräfin gave it to me. How generous she is. How I delighted in her company.

Through the window I see a carriage sweep up to the house. We have guests. I have Collette take Totworth out and have Clara assist me in dressing. Clara is most efficient. I descend the steps to the entry as our guests are being greeted by Sir Albert. They see me now. The man greets me graciously. His eyes linger on my thrusting breasts. The woman looks from me to her husband then back. She smiles and is most courteous. Sir Albert apologizes and makes formal introductions. He tells me he invited them before I even arrived, for he feared I might be bored. He would not presume to invite guests now. At least he knows who wields command in this house now.

The gentlemen and lady are neighbors, Edmund and Jane Bringham. Sir Albert says they have a fine home nearby. We visit and chat formally over tea and cakes in the West drawing room. These two interest me. They would have me visit them for a day or two. I sense they see in me the innocent. I can play such a part well when it is suitable.

"Could you come today, perhaps? We would so love to have you."

I blush and appear to hesitate. Then I acquiesce. They intend my seduction in some way, I have no doubt. I know the signs. It will amuse me to play the innocent. But in the end we shall see who seduces whom.

I leave Nannette and Clara in charge of Wellingham. They shall brook no affront to their authority. All shall be well in my absence. Collette helps me pack for a short stay—just a few days perhaps. Sir Albert will miss me, but I have left instructions as to his regular treatment, so he shall have his solace. The solace of being slowly teased to orgasm by knowing feminine hands.

I accompany Edmund and Jane in their carriage. It is a delightful coupe, all padded within in soft tooled leather and black velvet. I am placed between them. As the horses draw us on I am complimented and regaled from both sides. They would draw me in though I am not sure what they would draw me into. I decide, however, to play the game. I shall be drawn enough to find their puppet strings. Then it is they who may be drawn into a world of my fabrication where they have parts to play.

Edmund is courtesy itself, though he is most taken with my charms. His eyes linger and caress in a most ungentlemanly fashion. Jane sustains the conversation with anecdotes of charm and sophistication. I can learn from her. She is polished and cultured like a fine pearl from the Orient—lustrous milk-white perfection set off on an elegance of black velvet.

At last we arrive at their sumptuous home. We sweep up the drive and quietly efficient servants appear. There is a bit of unease in them. Somewhere deep inside they cringe when Edmund or Jane command. It is not overt, but still it is present. My stay shall be most enjoyable. I shall play the innocent to the hilt.

My room is exquisite and carefully furnished with every luxury. The Bringhams are wonderful hosts. I feel welcome. After I am settled we converse in a finely-appointed drawing room.

Jane talks of servants and the ever-present problem of discipline. I am attracted by her use of the word. I wonder why she chose this specific word when others would have done as well. There is promise in her choice of words. A hint of delights. I listen wide-eyed to their discourse. My acting is a success. They treat me as an intelligent equal. However, there is a hint of condescension, for they regard me as uninitiated. Jane asks if servants should be held accountable for their misdeeds.

"Most assuredly so. If they have in any way abnegated their responsibilities there must indeed be some form of retribution. The severity of such would be dependant on the extent."

"Would dismissal be too harsh a retribution?" Jane asks.

"Only those in authority can determine what is too harsh, or not. I am sure it is quite beyond the members of most household staffs to divine the heart of justice in such matters." I am plied with a fine liqueur. Gently I am steered to the position that servants should only be too grateful that whatever punishments they are given are not more severe. I make it clear that the problems of the less privileged are but a bore to me and of no concern unless they in some way affect my enjoyment of life. Upon this stand I am complimented. They both assure me that I am most perceptive.

Our conversations continue. We agree on much. We talk of the high calling of the few and how those who the world calls "privileged" are those with the heaviest burdens. I feel the beginning of boredom. I wait only for what lies ahead. For the delights their pompous words excuse and encourage. I stroke the stem of my wineglass with my gloved fingertip. I do not miss Edmund's stare. Is that a bead of perspiration on his brow? Perhaps in his imagination the stem of my glass is his swollen penis. I grasp the stem of my wineglass between my thumb and fingertip. I work it innocently with my fingers.

CHAPTER III

After a most satisfying dinner Jane plies me with questions in a small parlor. I begin to see the way of the Bringhams. The true structures of power are revealed. Jane is the master here. Edmund's power is but derived from her own. He is the planet in orbit of her sun. She is the center, the fountainhead of strength and imagination. Such is how it should be. When the dullard male is at the front there is but stagnation. The same old drives are but tiresome masters. When a woman wields command, however, there is no limit to her originality. Even the improvisations of the woman smack of true genius and mastery.

Jane wishes to initiate me into some mystery. I am invited to accompany her down a small hallway. We enter a luxuriously furnished room. Jane bids me sit down. The carpet beneath my feet is thick. Our footfalls are noiseless. The walls are upholstered in rich pink satin. The lighting in the room is from discreetly shaded lamps. The relatively small size of the chamber does not in any way detract from its loveliness. We are in a place of feminine confidences.

Art adorns the walls. Gilt-framed paintings of lovely young ladies in flowered hats with youthful lips that pout and smile. Two chairs face each other beside a thick velvet curtain that covers one wall. Handy to the chairs is a pedestal tray equipped with dainty glasses and a decanter of liquid refreshment. Nigh to the chair where Jane sits is a small table covered by a cloth. I sit across from Jane. An air of expectancy fairly hangs about the room.

"Nina, are you an adventurous young lady? Or is my assessment of you perhaps mistaken in some way." Jane looks at me closely. Her lips are pursed. Her brow is thoughtful. I respond quickly, scenting coming delights with an eagerness that I did not know I possessed.

"Oh yes, Jane," I allow myself to babble, remembering my role of unspoiled innocence ripe for unknown pleasures. "I do so love a thrill and have in fact never feared the unknown. Do proceed." I am truthfully dying to know what the curtain conceals. Jane reaches up and pulls a tasseled cord drawing the curtain open. I gasp.

Jane's eyes are upon me. My eyes are upon the spectacle the curtain has concealed. There in the wall before us is a circular opening gasketed by a heavy leather skirting. Kneeling through the opening is a naked male! From the shoulders upward he is hidden from our view as that part of him is in the space beyond. His back, waist, buttocks and legs are revealed to our gaze. His ankles are fastened hard down upon an oaken block with a strap and I surmise he is similarly constrained on the other side. I can see his testicles hanging exposed as well and allow myself to blush and then turn from him to Jane, my eyes wide and questioning.

"He is one of the servants, Nina," she says casually. "One who, I fear, must feel a taste of the tawse in order to remedy his behavior."

"The tawse?" I repeat.

Jane withdraws the cloth from the table, thus exposing is a thick strap of fine cowhide adorned with a smooth wooden handle. The strap is slit from its broad tip down one fourth its length. I cannot tear my eyes from it. How I want to wield it on the helpless buttocks before me until the poor wretch fairly sobs for my mercy. And then I would but begin anew. Instead I ask the obvious. "Are you going to see to him now? Here and now are you going to punish him?" My voice is thick with incredulity. Yet I also allow a hint of intrigued curiosity to seep into my words. Jane reads me well and sees the eagerness I pretend to hide.

"Yes, Nina, I will now strap him. Please watch and learn. A light hand is never an advantage when dealing with one's servants." With that Jane picks up the tawse and adjusts herself to sit forward on her chair so that she may have more freedom of movement. Then she raises the tawse and brings it down with a resounding crash upon the bottom of the helpless servant. Over and over again the tawse rises and falls, each time its point of impact controlled to perfection. The redness of each new stroke overlays the old by a third until the victim is decorated from lower back to top of thigh with ever brighter color. I watch in fascination. My quim fairly tingles with the enjoyment of the event. The leather skirting about the man's waist is thick, but I think I hear muffled pleas for mercy and am gratified that no mercy is given. Jane continues the strapping while addressing me. Her tone is calm and matter of fact.

"Nina, one's sensibilities should not be offended at the nakedness of the male during punishment. It serves two useful purposes. The first is to deprive the culprit of dignity and to prcss upon him thc unworthiness of his station. Secondly, any clothing present would but mitigate the pain which I wish him to experience in its full intensity." She continues the strapping, now creating a delightful cross-thatched pattern on the quivering buttocks. "The skirting serves to give privacy and anonymity to the disciplinarians. Such occasions for the disciplinarians should not be joyless events. They, unlike the culprit have committed no trespass. They may, and in fact often do, converse and enjoy refreshments from time to time during breaks in the procedure." I am amazed at Jane's revelations. I am in a perfect state of ecstasy, as the wetness between my thighs will attest. She continues. "Occasionally the victim may erect. On these occasions he should be subjected to indignities so that he will speedily unlearn such lewdness."

At last Jane is finished, at least for now. We sip tea and talk together. I shall reward Sir Albert upon my return. I will masturbate him over and over until he is glassy-eyed. How good of him to put me in touch with the Bringhams. How little he knew what pleasures would ensue. Jane tells me I must strap the servant next. I blush profusely.

"No, I'm sure I cannot. I have never done such a thing." Jane is most insistent. Reluctantly I concur and take up the strap. It is warm and smooth in my palm like a phallus. A phallus swelling with the longing to be pumped. I must keep to my role. I bring the strap down upon the servant's buttocks. A half-hearted stroke. Jane will have none of this. I am instructed in the proper severity. Allowing myself to slowly, then more quickly take up the rhythm of punishment, I advance. My tutor is pleased. Her eyes are bright and her cheeks flush as the strap lands viciously over and over again. After a dozen strokes I stop for a moment.

"Am I doing well? Am I properly applying the correction?"

Jane laughs. "Nina, you are indeed a quick study. Please continue. I believe you have a natural talent for the act of discipline. You have a gift."

Her adulation pleases me and I resume. The bottom before me is now excruciatingly sore, but I continue nonetheless. I lean forward as I apply the strap and press my legs together. I come as my swollen pussy lips press against the silken fabric of my undergarments. My clit is itching madly and I am suffused with a sudden heat. My eyes meet Jane's. She has the knowing. I throw down the strap and we embrace. She kisses me. I am flushed and hot. Her hands caress my breasts through my blouse. My nipples harden. I am quite swept away with emotion. Our lips meet in a lingering kiss. Jane's tongue probes between my lips and entwines with mine like a pair of snakes copulating. She squeezes my breasts again as I press against her. My hand drifts down her waist and hips. I wander lower and find the bottom of her skirts. I lift them slowly and run my fingertips along the inside of her leg up to her thigh. She moans and writhes in my grasp as I reach the top of her undergarment and worm my hand within. Jane opens her eyes in surprise, then smiles and resumes kissing me. She kneads my breasts as I massage the bounty of hair upon her mount. Two of my fingers inch toward her already-wet slit and separate the folds. I feel the warm hardness of her clit and roll it between my fingers. With my other hand I unbutton her skirts and draw them from her. A moment more and she is naked from the waist down. She smiles delightedly as I resume my fingering of her, putting my palm flat against her mount and insinuating two, then three digits in her slit. She moans and pushes her hips forward as I fuck her this way. I tease her clit as I continue to invade her passage. She is breathing deeply and a flush has risen to her neck and face. She cries out as her pearly juices begin moistening my fingers. I drive them in and out until her passionate murmurs subside. At last we draw apart. I straighten my hair. Jane pretends to pick a bit of thread from her skirt where it lays.

After a lovely breakfast of melons, tangerines and the lightest pastry imaginable, Jane and I continue our pleasurable activities. Of Edmund I have seen nothing yet today. Once again we walk the passage to the tawsing room and find this time a new miscreant ready for his reckoning.

A pretty maid accompanies us. Her name is Mary and I see in her much of what I have in Clara. An audacious and willing compatriot and, save for an accident of birth, an equal. We seat ourselves and make light conversation as we view the naked man fastened at the leather skirting. This one's legs are spread so that his cock is fully visible. I cannot seem to take my eyes from it. I would have him know the exquisite torment of being worked slowly to the ragged edge of spurting over and over again. I would adore having his organ twitch in my soft hand begging for release. Then I would apply the tawse slowly and with careful patience over his bottom. I would begin the cycle all over again. Jane's voice snaps me out of my reverie.

"Nina, I can see in your eyes what you long to do to him. You shall be given the opportunity. First, however, there is other sport planned. Mary, please prepare him for further humiliations."

Mary has withdrawn a wooden phallus from a wall cabinet. She oils it lightly then kneels behind the victim. Jane and I watch closely with great interest. Mary separates his bare bottomcheeks with her deft fingers and inserts the polished wooden phallus slowly with her other hand.

"Look, she is making his organ harden," Jane observes with amusement.

I crane forward to see better. Surely it is so. His organ is now vast and impressive. The head is purple and swollen and the shaft bobs to and fro. The phallus is fully inserted and the maid is dismissed. I watch the phallus slowly begin to slide from the man's bottom.

"Quick, Nina! Hold it in him lightly with your foot."

I respond. I raise my leg and bring the sole of my dainty shoe against the flat base of the phallus. I watch the satin bow of my high heeled shoe as I press my foot forward slowly. The phallus disappears into his bottom. I prod him a bit more by wiggling my foot. Jane is amazed at my taking to dominance so readily. She is pleased. She tells me to take my foot away. I do and the phallus slowly slides out of him and falls to the floor. I could see his buttock muscles tense in an effort to retain it, but to no avail.

Jane pulls a velvet cord. I faintly hear a distant bell. The maid returns. There is expectancy in her eyes. "Mary, he has expelled the phallus. He has been well instructed as to what he must do and he has failed'. "See if he is wet." Mary reaches under the servant and grasps his cock firmly. Then she slowly draws his foreskin forward. She rubs the thumb of her other hand over the slit in his cap. Her thumb is beaded with moisture.

"He is wet. May we punish him?" I enquire eagerly.

"Certainly, and you may do the honors, Nina," Jane declares charitably. Mary is dismissed and I take up the tawse. I kick off my shoes for better comfort and arch my silk-stockinged feet against the legs of my chair.

Again I set about the business of slowly tormenting a helpless male's backside. I am gratified to see his balls sway from the force of my blows and his penis, though remaining pendant, loses some of its girth from the pain. Jane watches me, her lips parted. Her eyes are swimming. My cleft is all inflamed. I strap the servant yet more severely in my delight.

"Nina, please kneel upon your chair as you tawse him," Jane breathes. I do so. Jane arises from her chair and stands behind me. I feel her gentle hand raise my skirts. I am naked beneath. I have discarded my undergarments in expectation of full enjoyment while inflicting punishment. She tucks my skirt up at the small of my back. My fulsome globes are revealed—bare to her gaze. My pouting cunt beneath beckons her hand. I am quite beside myself. I have never felt so utterly naked. The strap crashes on the servant's bottom with extreme force. I flail him cruelly in my excitement. Jane's fingers graze my lips. I am ashamed for her to find me so wet. She takes my clit gently between her thumb and forefinger and massages it. I orgasm immediately. My bottom quivers. She is not finished. As I continue to administer discipline she fingers my slit. Her forefinger strokes my lips while her thumb finds and probes my bottomhole. My anus contracts on her thumb and I come again. I am too weak to continue. We trade places. Jane takes up the tawse and I reach beneath her to rub her mount. With two fingers I knead and stroke her taut little clit, pausing from time to time to tease the sensitive edges of her lips. I work my fingers around the moist folds, probing and stretching as Jane continues the punishment. I mimic her actions, scouring her bottomhole with my thumb while I diddle her soundly. My hand feels locked in place by the tightness of her twin orifices. I jiggle it and am rewarded by a shudder that reverberates through Jane's body. She wets my hand with her juices in the delirium of her spending. She wiggles her blemishless bare bottom while cruelly flaying the same part of her helpless servant's anatomy. At last we finish. She drops the tawse and we embrace. Our gropings soon bring about another mutual orgasm.

I am mad to feel the servant's penis hot in my hand. I am desperate to goad his manhood from him in the spurts of humiliating submission. My clit feels swollen to vast proportions. Still holding my skirts up to leave my bottom bare, I kneel beside the servant. His ass is now heavily bruised. I reach beneath him to clasp his cock. It burns my fingers with the heat of his arousal. I reach under his bottom to grip his balls. I masturbate him with my other hand. I work his foreskin roughly to and fro. I find pumping a helpless male to be one of the sweetest pleasures. I never feel such a ripeness of desirable womanhood as when I am slowly draining a man of his strength. How I love to bathe my hands in the liquid heat of his weak surrender. The servant trembles mightily.

Reaching between his legs I start massaging his balls while my other hand skims his cockhead and works his shaft. I pump the turgid flesh up and down, admiring the way the head deepens in hue and the slit begins to gasp. He is so hot in my grasp that he fairly threatens to burn my hand; his tool pulsates with each fevered stroke. I squeeze his balls forcefully and slide my other hand to his helmet. I hold the slit open as he spends. I watch the torrent of his sperm spill through the air to spatter the carpet. I frig him afterward just enough to mock him as he is drawn, milked and exhausted. I stand up and wash my hands in a small silver basin affixed to the far wall. Jane and I set ourselves to rights and then leave the room to enjoy a fine luncheon.

Edmund joins us at the table. We eat and converse easily. Does Edmund know of the little room and its secret amusement? He must, although there is much of which the male may be kept ignorant. I watch Edmund closely. He is quietly gasping. Jane holds her fork in her right hand, but her left is concealed. She is diddling him at the table! Her fingers pull and prod his manhood even while he is forced to reveal naught but proper deportment. He removes his napkin from the table and pretends to place it in his lap. I giggle as he shudders.

In the afternoon Jane brings me upstairs. We walk down a long carpeted passage. She enters a door at the end of the hall and I follow. There in the room tied to the four posts of a bed is a lad of eighteen. He is stark naked. He is of average build and his skin is smooth and unblemished. His cock is long and thin and stirs as we rake him with our eyes. We move to his bed. We stand above him. Jane surveys him coolly. "He is my stepson. Edmund's child by his first wife—a woman of low breeding I am sure. He has returned home on summer holiday from Eton. They have filled his head with nonsense. He dreams of independence and fulfilling his destiny. Isn't it ridiculous Nina?"

"Simply ridiculous," I state agreeably. "Males should know their place and do as they are told by those who know better than they what is best for them."

"You would do well to listen to her, Reginald," Jane observes. "Feel free to examine him, Nina. He is well-hung for a male of his age, don't you think?"

I do think. I concur. We sit on his bed. I have the longing to feel him and manipulate him. He squirms in embarrassment, though his prick continues to move about and stiffen by slow degrees. He has no love for this. He would be master and yet he is the slave. How exquisite. How delightful. I lift his cock with my fingers.

"I have Mary see to him. She jacks him off once each day. How it galls him to come in her hand when he would much rather come in her pretty little pussy. Would you care to do him this time, Nina?" Jane offers generously. I assent. Jane tells me that he has not yet been milked today, so I should be gratified at the volume of his spendings.

I couch his balls on my palm. He has been shaved. He is as hairless as an infant. I can imagine Mary shaving him. Her fingers are skillful. His penis is hard and dripping moisture from time to time. Her smile is self-satisfied. He bites his lip at the indignity. Jane intrudes on my thoughts and says that he has to learn subservience. The subservience of being milked to weakness, then milked again. I tell Jane a bit about the Gräfin.

While I talk I hold Reginald's penis. I feel it slowly stiffen against his will. He is most mortified. I tell of a special jacket of heavy fabric that the Gräfin had her tailor construct. It was used to cover males from collar to crotch. The sleeves were extra long and attached to straps so that they might be wrapped about the person to be confined within. A narrow strap passed between the male's buttocks and divided itself to hold tight the base of the genitals. Then it came together again and buckled to the hem of the jacket just below the male's navel. Jane is fascinated and impressed by my casual discussion of such things.

"What was it for, Nina? Upon whom was it used?"

"It was used as a device of punishment and humiliation. The Gräfin had frequent parties for ladies only. Occasionally a male would be brought out so clad to amuse her guests. The women and girls could be quite merciless in toying with him. It was utterly forbidden for the male to ejaculate. The women knew this and often would frig the poor victim and toy with him most cruelly. They would pump his shaft and caress his balls, sometimes even going so far as to lick them. The males bit their lips and went through great contortions not to spend. It greatly amused the guests. Sooner or later someone's hands would work the male just a bit too much. He would moan in anguish and spurt thickly all down his legs and into the tormenting hand that shamed him. The younger women were most often guilty of this diversion. They took malicious delight in hearing the cries of the male later through the punishment room door as the Gräfin's maids repaid him for his crime. They could be very remorseless with the lash."

"Oh, Nina! What a capital idea! What perfectly excellent sport. What a fine plan for dear Reginald. I shall commission such for Reginald this very night. I shall have them finish it by tomorrow."

Poor Reginald is quite stricken. He glares at me helplessly for bringing this horrid idea to his stepmother's attention. I look down at him and smile cruelly. "Dear Reginald, I am so pleased you are horrified at such an excellent idea. Males never know what is best for them. Were you in agreement I should doubt the wisdom of this course." I grip his now very erect organ and work my fist up and down its length hard enough so his balls bounce against his bare bottom with every stroke. He tries manfully not to come. I laugh at his puny efforts and work him vigorously. I pump him up and down and move his shaft from side to side, slapping it occasionally against his belly. I bring him near to the brink and release his tool to twitch its pleadings against empty air. Jane and I converse and talk of upcoming social events. We discuss the betrothal of various notables and the activities of sundry noble personages

Then I return to work poor Reginald into a state of perfect frenzy. He does not wish to shame himself and spend in the hand of a pretty houseguest while his stepmother watches in amusement. Jane is impressed with my handiwork. She has me leave off the frigging a moment and she substitutes her hand for mine to try my technique. She pistons him hard and fast and suddenly bends her head and takes him in her mouth. Reginald groans as she licks the head all around until it assumes a wine-dark hue. He wishes her to continue, but suddenly she stops without warning. Then after a bit she has me resume.

"Have you licked and paid servile tribute to your pretty stepmother's bare bottom, Reginald?" I ask coyly. Jane blushes but there is intrigue in her eyes. "I fear he is going to spend, Jane, he twitches so much. What a mess he shall make if he does."

"Shame on you, Reginald, you wicked thing," Jane taunts. "I shall have you flogged if you come. The very idea. To think that you would even consider spurting into a pretty lady's hand who is just soothing you in your bound state. What foolery. You shall surely be punished if you spend."

I frig him more briskly. I fairly flog him now in my busy fist. He tenses and his sperm arcs out in long spurts. Even as he spends he hears our mocking giggles and assurances of eventual punishment.

After dinner Jane confides in me. We talk together of private things. Edmund has a problem that results in his sometimes being unable to express romantic feelings in a normal way. She is most discreet in her revelations. She tells me that I mean much to her and wonders if she can ask me for a special favor. I am all ears. She tells me of the writings of a certain Dr. Hutton. A very influential man. He is the same doctor who published a pamphlet for young men entitled *The Grievous Sin of Self-Defilement and its Unhappy Results*. Apparently Dr. Hutton believed that there was one possible cure for male impotence. It would require the services of a good friend of the man's wife. A female friend.

I listen wide-eyed. I allow just a touch and flavor of innocence—heretofore lost in the tawsing room—to slip back.

Jane takes a deep breath. "To sum up Dr. Hutton's rather lengthy article, he seems to indicate that if a friend of the wife holds the husband's balls during coitus, the sad effects of impotence can often be overcome. He states further that the best position for this is for the husband and wife to be upon their bed. The wife should be on all fours and the husband entering her from behind. In this way the female friend of the wife may sit in a chair next to the bed, and reach over to couch the husband's balls upon her palm."

We both flush. What a revelation! I have no idea whether or not Jane's story is true. Either way the tableau excites me. I picture it. I have to stifle the urge not to laugh. I assent. "Dear Jane, I should be most happy to help you and Edmund in any way. Even in an assistance of intimacy. You may depend upon my utmost discretion." She tells me that she will send Mary to me when all is ready. Then I should go directly to their bedchamber.

To amuse myself in the meantime I enter Reginald's room. A young maid sits upon the edge of his bed. She is washing his privates.

"Do you want me to leave, Miss?"

"Oh, no. Please continue your task. I just rather enjoy the sight of a young man humbled and in his proper place." The maid is pretty. Reginald's penis slowly hardens during the washing. Her name is Belinda, I think. I have intruded upon her private enjoyment. The private teasings and toyings she so enjoys. I pull up a chair near the bed. I do not sit down but rather I slip off my right shoe. I stand and rest my right foot on the cushion of the chair. I am on tiptoe. I hike up my skirts. The room's lighting enhances the texture of my fine lace stockings. I wear nothing above them. I pretend to slowly smooth them. Reginald's eyes are fixed upon my leg and foot. I know he can see the inviting shadow of my muff, though he doesn't let on with his eyes. His dancing prick is another matter. I have read him well. "Belinda, pump him a bit." The snap of command is in my quiet voice and she obeys.

She works him slowly. His eyes are fixed upon my lace-stockinged charms. Almost immediately she has him at crisis.

"Stop, Belinda. Else the little wretch will soil your hand." I wiggle my toes and slip back into my shoe. I turn and leave the room. I hear Reginald's groan of disappointment behind me. When I gain the end of the corridor I giggle. I cannot help it. A youth longing for his orgasm is deprived. What an amusement!

In my room I put on a dress of black velvet brocade. I leave on my knit stockings. I slip into dainty black leather shoes with black satin bows. One must dress discreetly for such things. One must always be proper even in one's dalliances. A few moments later there is a muted knock at my door. It is Mary. The time has come for me to join the Bringhams in their bedchamber. I follow Mary to the door of their room. She curtsies and departs. I knock gently.

Edmund opens the door. He is wearing a kilt in his mother's family tartan. He is wearing a shirt and waistcoat as well. He is most formal. I smile and almost laugh at him. Jane sits on the bed. She is wearing a tight corset and nothing else. Her hair is up and her pubic thatch is golden. She looks like an ancient queen. She should have dozens of naked male slaves to kneel before her. Their cocks would be swollen nigh to bursting with adoration.

She smiles at me and welcomes me. I kiss her cheek. The Bringhams do not waste time. Jane turns and kneels upon the bed, her buttocks shaped like a fine pear, ripe and curvaceous. Edmund gets up on the bed a bit awkwardly behind her. My chair has been positioned. I sit and Jane tells me to work Edmund to erection in my hand, then hold his balls while he penetrates her. I am blushing. I reach up under Edmund and encounter no undergarments. Beneath his kilt he is quite bare. My fingertips graze his thighs. In a moment I have hold of his balls. With my left hand I raise the front of his kilt and grip his penis. I tug him suavely and he begins to stiffen. Jane wiggles her hips. She has the longing for the penetration. Edmund's cock is hard and I guide it toward her pouting cunt. With a bit of help from my hand his head enters the slit. I watch the length of his organ slowly slide into Jane. At last her taut lips clutch at the base of his weapon. Edmund is like a statue. He is terribly embarrassed, yet I felt every beat of his heart in his organ when I worked it in my hand. I have only his balls now. Poor Edmund. He does not know what to do with his hands. He could rest his left hand on my shoulder but he does not feel free. He is so silly. I have his balls in my fist and he feels it improper to rest his hand on my shoulder. I giggle. He holds his hands awkwardly in front of his waistcoat. He looks rather ridiculous.

"Oh Edmund, work your prick in and out," Jane orders him crossly.

His hips move back and forth as he obeys her. My hand follows clasping his balls. I notice my skirts have slipped up a bit. Edmund can see my lace-stockinged thigh. I adjust my skirts modestly with my free hand. One must always be circumspect even when one is dandling the balls of another woman's husband upon one's palm.

Edmund is very busy now. He is pistoning in and out of Jane in accordance with her demands. He withdraws until his head is almost expelled, then enters to his full length again. My cheeks flush as I watch. There is a froth of passion juice on the lips of Jane's pussy. Edmund groans. He has maintained his hardness yet cannot seem to spend. Jane has come twice already and is urging him to pump her full of his sperm. I take the matter more in hand. I squeeze and twist Edmund's balls. I squeeze and twist until he throws back his head and goes all atremble. Then he rams his organ in her to the hilt and spurts again and again. Her cleft sucks his liquid essence as his eyes roll then twitch shut in intense delight. I pinch and slap his balls to aid his emptying. After he has come Edmund falls back exhausted. I daintily wipe my hand upon the coverlet of their bed. Jane thanks me profusely and says I am her ally. Edmund looks at me with fever in his eyes as I leave their room.

The next morning I am gratified to see Jane's tailors are true to their word. Jane has Mary bring me to the drawing room. There stands poor Reginald. What a sight! He is in a straight-jacket. His arms are fastened securely and his shaved genitals are goaded to hardness by the tight strap that encircles their base. Jane has him turn in order to exhibit his bare bottom with the tight strap visible between his bare cheeks. He dares not disobey. There is a choke collar about his neck attached to a leash. Belinda holds the leash. She looks quite proper and fetching in her lace apron and long ribboned cap.

"Oh, Jane, he is fabulous. What a curiosity! I do think such a garment becomes him. May I fondle him?"

"Of course, Nina. He exists but as a toy for our amusements. Even the maids handle and manipulate him. He is at your disposal." Mary and Belinda smile at the generosity of their mistress. I go to him and I lift his penis and rub it against his abdomen with the flat of my hand. He is agonizingly swollen and can barely contain his urge to shame himself. I roll his penis to and fro between his belly and my palm. "Jane, I recall you promised to have him flogged yesterday if he spent. I think perhaps his punishment is now due." I leave him and go whisper my plan to Jane. She giggles like a schoolgirl at its naughtiness. We implement my plan together. Jane sends Mary to pick fresh nettles. I have Belinda remove her undergarments in the hall. Upon her return I have her kneel upon the settee and raise her skirts to expose her plump bottom and lightly-mossed cunt. Jane and I force poor Reginald down upon his knees behind Belinda. He has great difficulty supporting himself as his arms are wrapped tightly about his own person by the jacket. Finally he is in place. Mary returns with the nettles and we have her stand behind Reginald. I bend down and take Reginald's chin in my hand. "Dear Reginald, you must now lick Belinda's bottomhole. You will lick her well while Mary lashes your posterior with the nettles. When you have licked her to her—and our satisfaction—your thrashing will cease. Such is the reward for naughty young men who spend shamelessly in the company of ladies."

Reginald is adamant in his refusal. His resistance but amuses us. The nettles fall upon his bottom leaving thin scratches. Mary is smiling in her work. She lashes him with the nettles again. Belinda looks back prettily over her shoulder to view the spectacle. Her face is aflame and her lips are parted in excitement.

Mary whips Reginald over and over with the nettles. Truly his buttocks must now be frightfully sore, but she does not desist. She has the enjoyment of punishment. There is none more merciless than a pretty woman who delights in the slow and gradual infliction of painful torments. At last Reginald bows his tear-streaked face to lick between Belinda's curvaceous bottomcheeks. She bites her lip with the pleasure of it and I can see her breasts rise and fall beneath her apron. She has turned away now and the contrast between her bare buttocks and proper attire on her upper half is most pronounced. The long ribbon that hangs from the back of her starched cap nearly tickles Reginald's nose. The nettles instruct Reginald well in the art of gently licking a woman's bottom. His red tongue is soon probing, then penetrating her anus. Belinda gasps and spends. Her bottom quivers and demands more adoration. I tell Mary to halt the punishment. She obeys instantly but I do not miss her disappointment. Jane and I watch as Belinda is licked to another orgasm. Reginald's tongue seems almost alive as it darts into her crevice and scours it clean. My pussy is now very wet. Jane's gaze is liquid as her eyes meet mine.

Belinda is soon fully satiated. She pulls down her skirts and gets up from the settee but remains to watch the sport. In sudden inspiration I slip off my shoes and draw down my stockings. I take them off and sit upon the settee with my legs crossed coyly. I make Reginald lick between my toes. It is a lark to have a spanked male paying homage to my feet. The Gräfin told me I have pretty feet and added I would enslave males with them. I did not then understand. Jane stands behind Reginald and raises her foot so the toe of her shoe bounces his shaved balls. She bounces them while he continues to lick between my toes. Belinda and Mary are fascinated observers. Then Reginald spends thickly upon the floor to our accompanying peals of laughter.

One afternoon several days later Jane and I sip tea on the south lawn and talk. It is a beautiful sunlit spot. We are languid and relish the discussion of many things. "I well remember the first time I ever masturbated a man," Jane ventures.

"Oh, please tell me! When did you discover your talent for such handiwork?" I enquire avidly.

She laughs at my curiosity to hear the details of such things. She sips her tea and dabs her mouth with her napkin. "It was a long time ago when I was full of the carelessness and haughtiness of privileged youth. I had not a care in the world and believed that everything existed but for my amusement."

"And so you are today; nothing has changed," I tease.

"Oh, Nina, do stop it and let me tell my tale," Jane chides. I listen as she resumes. "We had a young stableboy who was very shy. I think he was a bit in love with me at the time. At any rate, I was wont to bathe my feet and legs in a garden pool in high summer when the days were hot. I noticed the stableboy always found an excuse to be about when I was doing so. One particular day I was very interested to see a peculiar bulge in his trousers when he was nearby. Never being in any way reticent, I called him over to me and demanded he reveal the cause of his projection to my curious gaze. I must tell you that he jumped and seemed near ready to dare my anger with disobedience rather than endure such embarrassment. At last he complied, for I was rather forceful. There he stood with his trousers about his ankles. I soon realized I would prefer to see him completely naked and so demanded this. He removed his shirt—revealing a well-muscled chest and shoulders—and dropped his trousers. He was wearing nothing underneath in the manner of the low-bred, and his nice, thick cock shot out as if it were an uncoiled spring. I had to admire it, it was so long and smooth. It grew from a thick patch of curly hair that covered his mount and lower belly. As he stood before me I commenced to masturbate his waiting tool, much to his surprise and satisfaction. Men are really so predictable. Simply put your hand upon their cocks and they are yours to command. I continued tugging him steadily and enjoyed watching as his pole thickened in my hand.

"I was much amused as to how much evident pleasure my action caused him. Never have I felt such a sensation of power, Nina, as I felt then with the stableboy's prick in my hand. I worked him busily until his body shook all over and he spurted upon the grass. After that I must confess I milked him often until the grooms wondered why he was so pale and weak."

Jane accompanies me into the dining room for dinner.

We are flushed from our erotic conversations. Servants stand by obsequiously ready to fulfill our every request. Edmund is late. Jane is most annoyed with his inconsideration. She whispers a plot of mischievous revenge in my ear. I giggle for I cannot help it. The servants stand straight and attentive. They have wooden faces. It is well for them to be so. Else Jane would have them kneeling through the leather skirting for the slow flaying of their buttocks.

Edmund enters with apologies. His glance is nervous. Jane has mastery over him. His personality is as helpless to gainsay her as his organ is helpless to resist her coy handlings. I despise Edmund. Percy was born a ridiculous fop. Edmund could have been more but has allowed himself to be emasculated in a way. One feels amusement when toying with servile males, yet one must also despise them a bit as well.

Halfway through the second course Jane's plan unfolds. I can tell by Edmund's blank expression that she has undone his trouser buttons and is manipulating his tool. Males often go slack-jawed when they are handled and their faces often assume quite witless expressions. It is an amusement to watch their faces while one is rubbing their pricks. Jane has abandoned his tool for a time. She gives me the signal. She raises her wineglass, makes as if to drink and then sets it down again.

I have been placed directly across from Edmund for a reason. I smile at Jane's signal and conversation continues as usual. Beneath the table I slip off one shoe. I curl my silk-stockinged toes and rub them against the soft pile of the carpet a moment. Then I raise my foot and gently place it in Edmund's lap. I can feel his hard exposed organ against the arched sole of my foot. His expression is priceless!

Jane and I talk of indoor gardens and flowers. Edmund is in an agonizing dilemma. The lace tablecloth hides my foot and his cock from the servants and from Jane. He believes I have my stockinged foot in his lap without Jane's leave or knowledge. He is most smitten with the feel of my silken toes against his penis, yet he fears Jane may resume her handiwork at any moment and thus discover what transpires. Beads of perspiration are visible on his brow as I begin wiggling my toes.

Jane interrupts our discussion of enclosed gardens. "Edmund, dear. Are you feeling ill?"

He composes himself and manages a too-casual smile. "Of course not. I am fine."

Jane's eyes dismiss him and turn back to me and what hanging vines best grace enclosed garden windows. But her lips curl upward ever so slightly in the faintest hint of a triumphant smile.

I work Edmund with my unseen foot. He tries half-heartedly to push my foot away once, but I return to my task a moment later with more vigor. I shall never understand why a pretty woman's foot is such a talisman holding power over servile males. However, my lack of understanding in no way impedes my amusement with the fact. Edmund's balls are compressed against my heel and his shaft is flush against the ball of my foot. I have him near spending now. I can feel his prick hot and pulsating even through my stockings. I ask him a question to further addle him. "Edmund, what is your opinion of corner trellises?" He starts. He has been holding his fork in the same position for at least half a minute. He is quite transfixed and his knuckles are white. Jane turns her gaze and waits for his answer as well. Still my foot works him, up and down, urging the eruption from him.

"Well speak up! You are being rude to our guest."

Edmund stammers and I feel the little twitchings of his penis as it surrenders beneath my toes. He comes and I feel the warm thickness of it on my silk stockings.

I withdraw my foot and Jane pulls back the tablecloth. Edmund trembles. We laugh at his discomfiture and then he knows he has been the butt of our prank. We view his ejaculate thick and white upon his belly and waistcoat. Jane and I scold him soundly in front of the wooden-faced servants. Then Jane summons Mary to clean him and even she does not resist chiding him a bit. We leave him there to the embarrassment of having his intimate parts wiped clean by a pretty maid.

Jane and I retire to the drawing room. We sip a fine old Brunnello from Tuscany. I enquire if Jane has ever allowed a male to penetrate her bottom. She nods. "Has Edmund had the pleasure with you?"

"No, I somehow associate him with the more conventional pleasure, though you have seen the difficulty he experiences even with that. Occasionally one of the servants has been allowed access to my anus but only after he has been soundly tawsed and with the promise of a second tawsing afterward. It is well to see that males are made to submit whenever they have been allowed a pleasure, Nina."

I keep our conversation upon this subject until Jane seizes the bait I have been parading before her.

"Nina, have you ever had your bottom penetrated?"

"No, I certainly have not," I reply.

"Then it is high time that you did. I have a splendid idea. I shall have Reginald pleasure your bum tomorrow night if you assent and I shall birch him throughout to see that he is most compliant."

I blush demurely and make as if I am shocked. I insist I cannot allow such things. Soon, however, I "reluctantly" heed Jane's eager and enthusiastic pleas to introduce me to this pleasure. I relish the thought of having a male expend his strength in my bottom. How the woman quells the male in all facets of the sexual act. The male lies limp and drained afterward while the woman suffers no enfeeblement whatever, but sits laughing with the male's wasted vitality dripping from her hands, cleft, or anus.

The next evening I await Reginald's arrival in my room. I sit naked upon my bed. The Gräfin once had me sit in this same position. She made one of her servants frig himself to orgasm while kneeling naked on the floor before me. The Gräfin said it was a way in which the male expresses his adoration of the female. I watched with disdainful curiosity until he spilled his sperm in long arcs upon the floor. Then the Gräfin had Erna, her young maid, fasten him down upon the block for a long whipping. I was allowed to watch that as well. My reverie is interrupted.

I hear a tap on the door. Jane enters, followed by Reginald and Mary. Mary is leading Reginald by a leash about his neck. His hands have been tied securely behind him. His organ is hard. The helmet is red and swollen and I spy a drop of moisture at the tip.

"Belinda has been tickling him with a peacock feather for an hour to bring him to a fine erection," Jane explains. "He pleaded and begged for release, but she has a light touch and kept him yearning on the brink the whole while. He has become quite addicted to his handlings and ticklings. I dare say if a woman were but to draw off one glove in his presence it would excite him near to spending." We all laugh at Reginald's expense.

"He has a penchant for bare toes now too, Miss," Mary says addressing me. "Since your games with him, Belinda and I often tease him by making him suck our toes. It brings on a massive swelling in his privates and we giggle." We all laugh again. Poor Reginald is very chagrined.

We commence our proceedings. I kneel upon the bed on all fours. I arch my back so my bottomglobes curve seductively to Reginald's worshipful gaze. Mary leads him up upon the bed by his leash while Jane unwraps the birch from its saltwater-soaked felt covering. Mary then produces a small vial of oil from beneath her apron.

Mary oils her fingers and then gently applies the lubrication to my aperture. I sigh with pleasure as her fingers briefly invade my fundament. Then she applies the oil to Reginald's swollen organ. Her hands have him glistening with readiness in just a few moments. Mary then stands holding Reginald's leash to see that he is most obedient. The collar about his neck is very tight and I wonder idly if it chafes him. Jane stands behind Reginald with the long cruel birch in her hand.

"Very well, Nina. Are you ready for him now?" I assent.

Mary takes Reginald's penis in her free hand and brings it to the ring of my ass. She spreads my buttocks gently and I feel the torrid head of his cock against my clenched muscle. He is instructed to work his hips and his penis slowly invades my fundament. I am taken with a feeling of most delicious fullness as he is slowly and deeply absorbed into my bottom. My anus grips and clenches greedily upon his shaft. The initial stab of sharp pain subsides when he penetrates me fully. His belly slaps my buttocks once he is completely seated in my canal. As he is ordered to begin the sliding in and out, my nub swells and tingles in a most pleasurable fashion. My cheeks have become two hot coals. I open my mouth and sigh with the sensations. I wiggle my hips and bottom to impale myself more fully upon him. Suddenly I hear the swish of the birch through the air and the crack as it lands upon Reginald's backside. It is music to my ears; with the sting of each blow he thrusts further into my bottom as if to avoid the impact. Jane is most severe with his punishment and I am penetrated more deeply with every cut he receives. He pounds me mercilessly. His balls thud against my upturned cheeks with each stroke. At last I orgasm shamelessly over and over again as he thrusts within me. My clit is aflame and my pussy lips are greatly swollen. I gasp and mew in my delight. Then I feel his organ twitch and fill me with a thick warmth. I am nearly delirious with repeat spending.

At last Mary orders him to withdraw and I savor the feel of his penis slowly sliding from my backside. With a soft plop his head is expelled. I rest my head upon my hands and smile. I have quelled him with my bottom.

Reginald is taken away to be bound for the night upon a wooden stool in which a leather phallus has been fastened so it penetrates his bottom. It is best to keep males in their place.

Jane begs my assistance again in her relations with Edmund. I accomplish my toilette and dress quickly. I am satiated but shall enjoy the feel of Edmund's balls in my hand as he expels his sperm into his wife's quim. Jane is randy and ready for Edmund's penis to satisfy her. I have known more than one woman to have need of immediate satisfaction after birching a young man's bottom.

As we walk to Jane's bedchamber I contemplate Dr. Hutton and his cure for impotence. I wonder if all female friends of the wife are as willing as I to hold the husband's balls. It is pleasant though it makes one feel a bit like those who breed fine horses. If I had a stable full of slaves I would breed them. No stallion would impregnate a female unless his balls were in my hand. I have heard of such things before. Was it in some classic culture that pretty young girls would dandle the groom's balls on his wedding night as he took his bride's virginity? I have the image of it. Eager young hands pinching and squeezing as the groom thrusts. Piercing giggles and shrieks of laughter as sharp fingernails provoke his spending.

I am still thinking of such things as I couch Edmund's balls in my palm. Jane has stately buttocks and curving hips. She could quell a regiment with her backside. Edmund works his hips to slide his organ in and out of her pouting cunt. I can hear the liquid sounds of their joining. Jane's pussy is stretched wide by Edmund's thick tool. He rotates his hips as he fucks her, trying mightily to satisfy her. It is pleasing to be fully dressed while others are naked. I squeeze Edmund's balls and he spends. He grips Jane's hips and pulls her to him as he rams deep within. His eyes are haggard. His balls have a longing for my hands, for my gripping and squeezing.

CHAPTER IV

As we are at breakfast the following morning Belinda interrupts us. She informs Jane and me that one of the servants from Wellingham has arrived with a carriage to take me home. Belinda is to tell me that I have a guest from the continent.

The maids help me pack and I stand at the door where Eddington waits patiently. Jane's eyes are full of disappointment. It is well I have such an excuse. I would have ended my visit with the Bringhams soon anyway. I am full of new ideas and my own dominions beckon me. I assure Jane that we are fast friends and that we will see much more of each other—and so we shall. I kiss her on the cheek and promise her I will be the hostess when next we visit. Mary and Belinda curtsy as I step past them to the carriage. Reginald will be well taken care of though I have designs that may include him as well.

I have missed Eddington and his sturdy loyal ways. As he takes my gloved hand to help me into the carriage I look full at him. There is adoration in his eyes. I smile and pat his cheek. I would like to stop on the way back to Wellingham to masturbate Eddington. His tool must long for my hands to work it—but I am pressed for time. I am most excited to see who my guest may be. Eddington has been sworn to secrecy.

When we arrive I see another elegant carriage at the front of the house and two freight wagons beside. In the hall I am greeted by my dearest friend of all. I cannot believe my good fortune! It is the Gräfin's maid, Erna. At Schonring she was my friend, confidant and compatriot. A maid, yes, but so much more beside. Within her breast beats a heart full of proud feminine strength. The Gräfin herself recognized a kindred spirit within her. Erna and I became fast friends in my months at Schonring castle and she taught me much.

We embrace, kiss and laugh upon each other's shoulders. She has the same youthful red-lipped smiling mouth and laughing eyes. She is not inclined to fat at all; her body is graced with the most delicious curves. Often the

Gräfin's male servants beg her for the privilege of covering her smooth calves with kisses after she has beaten them soundly. Afterward she prods them to spurting with her bare toes.

She tells me that she may stay as long as I have need of her services. She also tells me that the freight wagons are full of gifts that I may find useful. We are interrupted by a knock on the door. Clara admits Nannette. I am so glad she has stayed on and tell her so. The coming weeks hold many pleasures for all of us.

Erna, Nannette, and I take tea in the flower garden. I say what has been on my mind for some time. "It seems that in the disciplining of the males in this household I have been sometimes too playful. One cannot expect them to profit by light-handedness. I feel it may be time to take them more firmly in hand for their own good."

Nannette and Erna heartily concur. Erna tells me that I shall find the Gräfin's gifts of much use in this respect. They have been unloaded from the freight wagons and stowed in the rear of the carriage house. The three of us go to view the gifts and I am pleased. I have Clara and Collette alert the household staff. Two punishment rooms are to be set up, one downstairs and one upstairs. These rooms shall be equipped with the implements of discipline the Gräfin has so graciously supplied. They shall also be equipped with every comfort and luxury the female disciplinarians will need to sustain themselves through long hours of administering correction to those males found to be recalcitrant. Over the next few days discreet workmen are procured and my instructions are carried out to the letter.

Clara is glad to have me back and I must confess it does me good to see her pert freckled face and eyes full of mischief. Sir Albert is quite overcome, and though the maids have him well milked he is most rapturous at my return. What silly affectionate creatures males are! Even Totworth hangs about more than is usual. Collette has blossomed into a more confident woman and carries herself now with grace and dignity. I like to think it is at least partly due to my tutelage. Percy pretends to be ill and in good time I shall give him a cure that he may not like, though at least when he is about he now knows his place.In my absence I received another letter from Aunt Judith. I read and find it full of affection and family news. The last lines take my attention.

> *As you know, Nina, I have a generous traveling allowance from Sir Albert. I find myself in a constant whirl of parties and gaiety. I shall not soon return when there is so much fun to be had here along the Loire. I must confess—though by now you must realize, Nina—that I did not marry Sir Albert for any great love of him, though I do feel fondness and warmth. Some arrangements are best left in a more unconventional sense. I must say, Nina, you probably have the household firmly under your thumb by now. I would love to see it! We both have our own amusements. With love and fondest regards,*
>
> *Your Aunt Judith.*

My smiling perusal of Aunt Judith's words is broken by Erna who enters to tell me that the Gräfin has sent a male servant for me. His name is Horst and he is of splendid physique, she says. Erna has him toiling now pruning hedges in the back acreage of the estate. She says he is heavily muscled and has such endurance that one can pump him—or fuck him—nearly all day. It is fine sport. We both laugh.

My mornings back at Wellingham begin with more diversions. Nannette, Erna and I are in my personal drawing room. Erna is briskly efficient and ready for the day as usual. Clara has my hair down and is combing it carefully. Collette is performing the same services for Nannette. I have another maid summon Horst. I tell her to bring him to us naked so that we might have a look at him. Our conversations continue on a light vein until his arrival. The young maid who has escorted him is blushing furiously. Indeed, she blushes with good reason. He is an excellent specimen of virility. Five pair of feminine eyes linger most boldly and improperly upon him. He lacks Eddington's height, but he is heavily muscled all over. His shoulders and upper arms are massive and his chest promises great strength and endurance. His stomach is flat and hard without an excess ounce of fat. Our eyes linger lower. His organ is massive and erect and surrounded by a thick growth of curly hair. It is the cock of a bull or a stallion, certainly not that of a man. The shaft is long and amazingly thick. I doubt I would be able to close my fist around it. It is lined with dark veins that seem to pulse with energy. The head is enormous. I look more closely. When I collect my thoughts enough to speak I exclaim, "He has no foreskin, Erna! What has happened to him?" My eyes linger on his totally exposed and very swollen cockhead.

"The Gräfin was angry with him over a lack of control," Erna replies. "I recall she had him in a wheeled masturbation box for one of her lady friends to toy with. Horst became overexcited and spurted before the woman was through manipulating him. His sperm shot forth like a geyser and spattered against her mouth and chin before subsiding and pumping in a steady stream all over her hand. The Gräfin became angry and felt if his foreskin were removed he would receive less sensation from handlings and so hold his spendings for a longer time."

Horst's face is that of a blond youth with a look similar to Totworth's, yet more chiseled and bold.

"Why, that makes perfect sense, Erna." This from Nannette, who has called Horst closer and begins rubbing the shaft of his tool. "Perhaps I should have this done to Percy. He is quite selfish in his pleasures at times."

I ask Erna to tell how she and Horst first met the Gräfin. It is an amusing tale that I am sure Nannette would love to hear. As the maids continue their ministrations, Nannette and I handle and examine Horst's shaft and balls. I stroke him gently, enjoying the way his enormous tool throbs in my hand. Erna begins her story.

"When I was a young girl in Bavaria may days were filled with herding and milking goats. In the afternoon I would often have a bit of time to walk on the lower slopes of nearby mountains and bathe in the cool streams. One beautiful afternoon in high summer I was picking flowers when one of the boys from the village below came walking toward me. He asked if he could talk with me and so we struck up a casual acquaintance. However he soon became rather coarse and rude in his insinuations. He said he wanted me to take his cock in my mouth, or allow him to fuck me. Either would suffice. Well, I had no choice but to take him into a nearby copse of trees and tell him to uncover himself below the waist. I then told him to lean with his palms flat against a nearby tree and his buttocks thrust out bare behind. I broke off a supple limb and chastised him well with it until his bottom was red and sore. To my surprise he was most compliant through the entire procedure and quite meek afterward.

Soon other village boys would join me in my meadow walks—always one at a time—and they would soon beg me to whip them as I had the first. I refined my methods somewhat after the first episode. I would have the boys strip themselves naked for their punishment. I now carried a small goat whip instead of trying to obtain a branch. The boys would stand naked, buttocks thrust outward behind, palms flat against a tree trunk. I enjoyed seeing their young cocks dangling between their legs...though they were usually hard even during my harshest ministrations. I soon came to take active pleasure in my role of village disciplinarian and sent the boys home with bruised bottoms covered with stripes."

Nannette has a finger in Horst's bottomhole and he is working his hips to and fro while the maids watch in fascination. I have his penis clasped in my fist and am squeezing it to watch the head swell purple and huge. Nannette begs Erna to continue her tale.

"One particular afternoon several village boys brought me this one lad and told me that he needed a sound thrashing. They then listed a summary of his offenses and asked me to apply his correction with a will. They brought thongs and helped me strip him and tie his wrists to a low tree branch above so that he might hang helpless. Then they returned to the village asking me to address his correction for at least an hour. I must confess that having a victim so helplessly bound as he and having great leisure for the slow infliction of punishment delighted me. When I finished his bottom was decorated with horizontal, vertical and diagonal stripes and beginning to bruise nicely. His cries of pain were unheard by anyone but myself and I rather enjoyed the sound of them. At this point I noticed that his penis was engorged and for the first time felt a curiosity and a desire to touch a boy there. I cautiously reached over and touched him with my fingertip. Despite his pain he jigged his hips and I could tell that I had caused him a rather intense sensation of pleasure. He began begging me to touch him again. At last I took his penis in my hand and pulled the loose skin to and fro along its length. This sent him into a perfect agony of delight and he squirmed in his bonds and bit his lip. I worked him faster and faster, hardly knowing what I was doing, until he went rigid. My hand was suddenly filled with a thick warm flood of pearly fluid. I was fascinated at this and rubbed it about on my hands and played with it. I finally wiped it off upon the grass. I then felt he had been wicked to do such a thing in the hand of an innocent girl, so I began his punishment anew."

"As I was applying the goat whip to his hindquarters I heard a noise behind me and turned about. There upon a great white horse sat the most beautiful young woman I had ever seen. Her hair was golden and up in a tight bun. She wore a flowing white blouse. Her gloves, tight riding breeches, and high boots were all of black leather. I was in awe of her. She dismounted and came toward me with a riding crop in her right hand and a smile on her face. She patted my cheek gently, then turned to the boy that I was in the process of disciplining. She gave him three dozen hard cuts with her riding crop. He was nearly beside himself by then. She asked my name, mounted her horse and wheeled away uphill at a fast gallop. That was my first meeting with the Gräfin. Our victim, as you may have guessed, was Horst. The very next week she sent for us both to serve her."

"What a perfectly charming story!" Nannette declares. She has goaded Horst nearly to crisis now. I have her stop. I thank Erna for her tale and ask Clara to procure a pink ribbon from my dressing table. I have her tie it about his balls. I love the sight of it. The pretty pert-faced maid in black and crisp white lace tying a pink ribbon about a naked man's plums. I have her lead him about the room by it. He is most obedient with his organ straining before him. I have Clara make him get down on all fours and lick her feet like he is a cleaning machine. We all laugh as the dainty maid degrades him. It is most fetching how the pink ribbon leads from her hand to his hanging sac. I have Clara make him stand up. I go to him and support his penis upon my left palm. I spank the shaft lightly with my right hand. I spank it until it twitches and then it spurts. We watch the thick strings of his sperm spill out upon the floor. Nannette's eyes are wide and her mouth drops open.

During lunch Nannette tells me that Percy has become more uppity of late. He is such an insufferable bore! I instruct the servants to fasten him in the first floor punishment room. It is high time he was seen to. Nannette, Erna and I continue our lunch. When we are finished eating I summon Clara and Collette. With Nannette's full conniving we plan her husband's humbling.

His reckoning unfolds like clockwork. Nannette and I enter the enclosed side gallery of the punishment room. It is equipped with peepholes at regular intervals to allow viewing within for those who themselves wish to be unseen. We recline on velvet couches in luxurious comfort to see the spectacle before us. The punishment room has been furnished according to my specific instructions. No detail has been overlooked.

Percy stands with his hands suspended above him by leather wrist cuffs fastened to a fixed ceiling cord. His ankles are restrained by short lengths of cord attached to recessed rings in the floor. This is to dissuade him from kicking his legs during his ordeal. He is gagged by means of a wooden ball secured by a leather strap across his mouth. He is naked, of course, as all males should be to receive proper punishment.

I look at Nannette. She is most eager to see her husband taken down a peg or two and rightfully so. Percy is truly a ridiculously impertinent fop. One just naturally has the desire to humiliate and punish him. Nannette smiles at me. Impulsively I kiss her lips, darting my tongue into her mouth. Collette and Erna enter. They have donned severe dresses of grey wool with turned-back cuffs, high collars, and narrowly-spaced black buttons. Both wear short white aprons of frilly lacework. Both wear black stockings and black buttoned shoes. They wear gloves of white cotton and hold long feathers in their hands.

I have deemed it effective for Percy to have his punishment at the hands of the maids. Nannette and I have chastened him but he will feel the shame of it more when his pain is inflicted by servants. I have instructed them to draw it out so that he may feel every tickle to its full degree. Poor Percy! It is impossible for him to manage any semblance of dignity. His prick and balls are bare and he does not have enough leeway with his bound ankles to twist his genitals away from their casual gazes. He is quite humiliated! Nannette and I laugh together and I slip my arm about her trim waist.

Erna addresses the victim. "Percival Archibald James Wellingham. For lacking proper humility and for the crime of disrespect to the fair sex, you are hereby sentenced to numerous swishings with the feather across your posteriors. You must learn your place sir!" He almost looks relieved, for what discomfort could be caused by a mere feather. Little does he know! Nannette and I watch as we kneel upon the velvet couches, our arms about each other.

Both Collette and Erna stand behind Percy, one to each side. They begin. The feathers brush his bare buttocks with great vigor. Collette slowly works down his right side from his lower back to the back of his knees. Erna slowly works up his left side from the back of his knees to his lower back. Since they work on opposite sides in opposite directions they both can bring simultaneous strokes down upon him. The tickling is not forceful, yet his bottom starts to turn a pale rose shade. Both women bend at the waist and put the full strength of their hips and bottoms into it. Percy's smile now fades and becomes a look of concern as his bottom warms. The flesh is reddening and the tears in his eyes are not of joy. Soon he begins to jerk spasmodically against his bonds as the punishment continues mercilessly.

Strangely, Percy's cock is erect, though the sensitivity of his buttocks must be excruciating. Nannette and I are both flushed and breathing heavily at the sight of it.

Percy strains, writhes and squirms his muffled pleadings, but to no avail. His tormentors chat casually while sipping a bit of sherry for refreshment. They continue tickling his now-raw bottom with the feathers then they leave the punishment room and come to the gallery where Nannette and me await the next phase. Erna and Collette draw off their gloves and raise our skirts up behind as I have instructed them to do. Both are flushed from such good healthy exercise and are stifling their laughter. Nannette is shocked to feel Erna's hands upon her bare bottomcheeks. Her eyes are wide and she looks at me questioningly, but with more than a hint of enjoyment. Erna fingers Nannette's slit gently while Collette inserts her forefinger to the knuckle into my fundament. Then she wiggles and churns it, causing me sensations both delicious and poignant. We watch the scene before us in the punishment room while the fingerings continue.

Clara enters the chamber. She is wearing a leather singlet that is tight about her waist and leaves her bottom bare. She also wears elbow-length kidskin gloves. How impudent she is! Other than these brief garments she is naked save for a leather apron covering her front from her waist to her knees. Her buttocks and the back of her thighs are totally bare save for two thin leather straps to secure her apron, one just below her bottomcheeks and the other at mid-thigh. She turns about in front of Percy and bends over to begin a regimen of exercises. As she touches her toes and flexes her legs, her bottomcheeks thrust at him most alluringly. Despite the pain of his recent punishment he is soon very attentive to the lithe gymnast so bizarrely clad before him. The hidden gallery overlooking the punishment room is soon filled with stifled giggles as we watch his cock rise still more and thicken in shameless tribute to Clara's bare charms. How spineless males can be! One can rob them of all dignity and subject them to any pain as long as one teases their organs afterward.

Clara turns about to view the effect of her enticements on her victim. "Oh, your prick is all swollen, Percy. I hope I haven't caused it, but you see this room is also used for exercise. I see no reason to forego my routine just because you need a little discipline," she purrs. Percy is helpless like a boy whose organ is twitching and swollen from his teacher's slow teasing. Clara turns about again and bends over. She reaches behind to pull her bottom-cheeks apart—standing on tiptoe. She flexes her anus to his wide-eyed astonishment. "I could relieve your swelling Percy," she coos. She backs up to him and wiggles her bare bottom against his organ. She briefly grasps him so his cockhead is barely beginning the penetration of her butthole. "Let's play a game, Percy. I can make your poor organ feel so good! You can work it back and forth in my bottom as much as you like without penalty. If you spend, however, it would warrant a beating from me with a knotted whip on your already anguished buttocks and thighs."

Percy is frantic and tries to thrust into the maid's bare bottom. His wishes are clear. His motions are limited so she backs up against him and wiggles her hips until his cockhead is lodged inside her slit. Then Clara leans forward until his penis almost slips out altogether. Then she goes back hard against him on tiptoe over and over again. She is completely in control, adjusting the tempo to her own satisfaction. Percy hangs there, his face flushed and glistening with perspiration, pumping feebly. At last he senses his upcoming crisis. He tries manfully to withdraw. He knows the price he will have to pay if he comes. Clara giggles maliciously and her bare bottom follows him back, her anus clenching greedily and seated firmly upon his prick. With a groan of panic he ejaculates as her bottom sucks at him. Clara's face is flushed and her lips are parted. How she enjoys her role of tormentor! She slides away from him before he finishes spurting so the last of his sperm splashes thickly across her bare buttocks.

"Shame on you, you nasty thing! Now you shall have

the thong!" Nannette and I spend together from the maid's prolonged fingerings as Clara eagerly makes good her threat.

The next morning I prepare legal documents for review by my attorneys. I have decided to publish advertisements in certain periodicals for the well-bred that offer the following service: "Comportment and demeanor training for young gentlemen, ages eighteen to twenty-one." I shall also make discreet inquiries as to the offering of grace and confidence training for a select few fine young ladies. I shall teach the young women the art and skills of domination. The world has suffered long enough under male control. The young gentlemen will soon be putty in the hands of newly-confident young ladies.

The afternoon is a time for more amusements. Nannette and I enter Sir Albert's room. We have confined him within for a few days due to no trespass on his part—rather just to remind him of his place. Nannette and I both feel real affection for him, however, and it is high time we saw to the relief of his male needs. He, like the other males, has been strictly warned of any masturbatory behavior and threatened with a punishment akin to Percy's if he so indulges. By now of course, word of Percy's fate has spread like court intrigue. Clara thrashed him so well I would have thought she had long, careful training under a most accomplished flagellant.

Nannette and I sit in Sir Albert's dressing chairs. We have him doff every stitch of his clothing. He kneels before us, his whiskers fairly twitching in his eagerness to have his balls relieved. I have him lie down with his head beside my feet. I have previously removed my lace stockings. I command him to lick between my bare toes. I love a male tongue working between each one in turn. I smile down at him gently as he complies. Sir Albert is upon his back. Nannette slips off her buttoned pumps. Her silk-stockinged feet are daintily arched upon the carpet and most alluring. Of course her naked muff is visible beneath her skirt. Sir Albert clearly enjoys the view.

She has her toes curled into shimmering silken fists.

Perhaps I understand more why so many males have a great urge to worship women's feet with servile tongue and lips.

"Nannette, I am sure Sir Albert would love the feel of your stockinged toes working his foreskin."

Nannette giggles in response. She extends first one foot and then the other, her toes now pointed like a ballerina's. Sir Albert's organ is already turgid. He is unable to keep it soft while his tongue is sliding about between my toes and his eyes are glued to Nannette's cunt.

Nannette sits and clasps his penis firmly between the soles of her stockinged feet and rolls it about quite casually. In the meantime she adjusts her satin cuffs in an almost bored fashion. Sir Albert's face looks as though he is being subjected to slow strangulation. He sucks my toes with famished lips. His face reddens and he trembles. Nannette is now kneading his prick between the balls of her feet with a pouting expression on her face. She twists one lock of her hair about her left forefinger and moves her right hand so the ruby stone in her ring catches the light.

Sir Albert nurses at my toes. His organ is swollen huge now, the head an angry purple. Nannette's toes slide the sensitive skin of his foreskin up and down the shaft of his tool. She is quite shameless and immodest. Her skirts have worked well up upon her thighs and she is uncaring.

Sir Albert is moaning nonsense now, "Oh, I cannot...I mustn't....Oh, do cease at once..." His voice is muffled by a mouthful of wiggly toes. His tool expands between Nannette's tormenting feet. We both watch the white liquor brim from the slit in his cockhead and pour in a thick flow like icing down the sides of his knob and on down the shaft of his prick. He also generously soils Nannette's silk stockings. Laughing, we leave him there gasping upon the floor.

I have decided that Totworth may need a smart reminder of his status in order to assure his conformation to the new Wellingham order. Erna has planned for him an excellent exercise that I myself quite look forward to as well. I join Totworth and Erna in the upstairs punishment room.

I have tried not to equip the discipline rooms in a fashion that would make them appear too medieval. I have attempted rather to furnish them with the proper blend of luxurious comfort arranged about implements of punishment—to inculcate in the female an attitude of casual relaxation, and in the male, one of uncomfortable apprehension.

At my instruction Totworth kneels naked upon the carpeting. A leather covered post has been placed in a socket embedded in the floor behind him. Fastened about the post is a length of firm twine, the other end of which has been looped securely about Totworth's shaft. A comfortable upholstered settee has been placed in front of him. Erna stands primly behind Totworth holding a long, wicked birch.

"I am sure this will amuse you, Miss. This is one of the Gräfin's favorite games and it has found much use at her parties."

I pause by Totworth and have him kiss my hand. "Thank you, Erna. I am sure I shall find it entertaining." I remove my shoes and stockings, then sit upon the settee facing Totworth. I draw up my skirts and raise my bent legs such that my bare heels rest upon the edge of the seat cushions before me. My cleft is exposed naughtily, though Totworth wisely keeps his gaze well lowered. His penis is half erect as if in hesitation as to whether to swell or shrink small and await later pleasures. Male organs are fascinating to me in the way of a small helpless pet that one doesn't know quite whether to caress or tease. Handling a spurting organ that one has subjected to slow toyings is a diverting pastime.

I spread my legs a bit further and anchor myself well with my heels. I then bid Erna to begin. Without warning she lashes Totworth's bare bottom with a vicious cut from the birch. Before he can react he has received another blow and then another still. The fourth, fifth and sixth cuts also follow with great rapidity. Totworth winces and cries out in pain and surprise.

"Crawl to her and lick her well," Erna commands coolly, still continuing the birching of his posteriors. "The blows will not let up until you reach her and please her between her legs with your tongue."

Totworth obeys with alacrity but finds he is just short of his goal with the twine now fully extended. The cord pulls his stiffening cock down between his legs. Erna redoubles her efforts to flay his bare bottom. The long birch twists as it fairly whistles through the air.

"Continue, sir! The twine will stretch. Don't mince! Your cock will stand a little pulling, or you shall have no bottom left if it won't!"

Erna drives Totworth ever forward. He is quite between a rock and a hard place but at last his mouth reaches me. He groans and begins the licking. I look over his back and buttocks to see the twine stretched tight as a harp string. Erna has driven him until his tool is pulled back against his balls. It cannot be too painful—he is almost fully erect with the excitement of it all. She nudges the twine a bit with the pointy toe of her high-heeled shoe. It only vibrates, it is so taut. I laugh with the amusement of it. What simpletons men are. Possessed on the average with a greater physical strength than the female, yet they emasculate themselves willingly if one knows the skillful operation of their puppet strings. Erna has nearly ceased his birching now and only gives him an occasional reminding cut to keep him at the full extent of the twine and to assure the continued busy employment of his lips and tongue between my legs. She witnesses all, her cheeks flushed with satisfaction.

Totworth has been gently licking up and down my pussy lips, first one side and then the other. He slowly works me to near spending and in his discomfort has not forgotten his skills for such things. I rest my hands upon my knees and lean forward a bit to watch his tousled head bob between my thighs. I feel hot and wonder idly if I am showing the glow of perspiration. Totworth now deliciously licks my clit, his tongue at first tentative and then more bold as it slides wetly about. He licks it from side to side and then up and down, and then in spirals. I am quite beside myself now, though I do not reveal the full extent of my pleasuring. "Nibble it, you cur. Take it between your teeth and nip it, bite it gently," I command him. He obeys and I come in intense quiverings liberally salting his lips and tongue with the effusion of my spendings. I orgasm again and then he works lower and licks about my slit. He flicks at the inner folds and turns back the pink, conch-like flesh by pressing his mouth hard against me. At last he thrusts his tongue deep within me and wiggles it about. I nearly swoon with orgasms that follow one upon the other.

Totworth has satisfied me well. He still licks me gently and remains at the end of his tether. It amuses me and adds to my pleasure to think how sore his cock must be. Erna stoops down and her hands reach under and beneath his buttocks. I watch and cannot see what she is doing, though I can see that her wrists are moving busily. Totworth's hot, gasping breath warms the thatch of my mount. Erna continues her unseen ministrations and in but a few moments Totworth trembles mightily. Erna stands up flushed and giggling. Her hands are dripping with his sperm and her forearms are even splashed a bit with the thick liquid of his shame. My, but Totworth is copious today! I must whip him to the end of his cock leash more often. I spend again upon his tongue.

After our interlude with Totworth we proceed to other things. I have determined it will be beneficial if all the maids can view a male being humbled by women. I so arrange it. I have the maids assemble in the upstairs hall. Eddington is also present at my bidding. If the maids see such a fine strong specimen as he humbled it will reinforce in their minds who is master at Wellingham once and for all.

There before the maids I have Eddington remove all his clothing. His every move is watched by eager eyes. When he at last stands naked and exposed I see a red flush upon many cheeks. I survey the maids. Sir Albert has chosen well. They are all young and attractive, though Clara and Collette stand out as exceptional. I have Nannette lead Eddington by his now-erect penis over to the assembled maids. His shaft is thick and seems to jump in her hands. She stops by the first. They form a line with Collette and Clara the last.

"When he stops beside each of you I want you to reach out and gently handle his prick for a moment," I say. "You will find it will not cause you any pain or discomfort. Observe how easily Nannette works him in her hands." It is true, Nannette slides his foreskin readily to and fro. Her hand is tiny upon Eddington's girth, yet easily subjugates him.

"You will find the fabled monster that dangles between a man's legs to be but a puppy for the stroking hand," Nannette adds primly.

Several of the maids laugh. One by one they reach out and make manual acquaintance with Eddington's tool. Some clasp it briefly, blushing furiously, but others are far more bold and work it about avidly. Eddington stands ramrod straight and tries to compose himself as his swollen organ is well masturbated by all. One Irish kitchen maid with flaming hair takes delight in the weighing and handling of his sac. By the time she is finished a glistening bead of his arousal decorates her lace wristcuff. She smirks with amusement and a touch of pride.

I dare not let Collette finger him for fear of his being over-excited and spending. Rather I have him bend over and have her insert first one finger and then two into his bottomhole. She takes readily to this and probes him vigorously. The maids laugh as his prick bobs in time to Collette's casual fingerings. Clara is last in line and I must have something special for her to perform upon him.

On sudden inspiration I have him get down on his hands and knees on the hall carpeting. I have Clara remove her shoes and cotton stockings. I help her pull up her skirts and tuck them into her apron strings. Then I tell her that Eddington is her steed and she should exercise him by riding him up and down the hall. Her eyes flash with pleasure as she mounts her patiently quiescent beast. She sits well back upon him. I fashion a makeshift bridle for her of the lace ribbon from one of the other maid's caps. Nannette leans forward and slaps Eddington's bottom for Clara and they are off. Down the hall he goes at full gallop with Clara sitting coyly upon him. She reins him in and turns him about at the landing of the east stairway. Back and forth they go. The hall echoes with feminine laughter at the spectacle of it. Clara, giggling leans well forward and jerks the bridle to spur her steed on to greater effort. Poor Eddington is quite exhausted from the speedy transport of his unaccustomed burden. Clara will have no shirking. She slaps his buttocks smartly and pummels his swollen cock with her bare heels causing it to slap against his belly. Poor Eddington has been rather overstimulated I fear. The contact of Clara's heels upon his turgid meatpole induces his crisis. With an embarrassed groan he erupts in long thick arcs upon the carpeting. His prick bobs and jerks as it releases its load.

I angrily berate him for his lasciviousness. "Nannette and Erna, please see to him in the first-floor punishment room. Let Clara watch if she so desires. Apparently he needs a lesson in self-control."

They take him to the chamber. Nannette and Erna plot something special that they feel I will much appreciate. They have Eddington lie on his back in the center of the room. They remove his clothes until he is totally naked. Then they each put a hand on his cock and balls and begin massaging him to erection. They are gentle but persistent. His balls jiggle about under their ministrations and in no time at all his staff is twitching and stands fully erect. With a smile and a nod in my direction, Nannette suddenly straddles the throbbing cock and lowers herself upon it. Eddington's eyes widen in surprise, then he lies prone and enjoys his punishment.

It is destined, however, not be be what he expects. Nannette rides him and grinds her bottom against his thighs. His tool is lodged deeply inside her cleft. She pumps him avidly and the indiscreet smile upon his face signals to me that he is deriving too much pleasure from the activity. It will not last. Nannette fucks him until he is just about to spurt, then dismounts her steed. His sperm arcs into the air and splashes upon his belly and the floor.

As soon as the spasm subsides, Erna is upon him. She grabs his still-turgid shaft harshly and stuffs it into her demanding pussy. Eddington continues to smile, unable to credit his good fortune. Erna rides him much as Nannette did, only as she does so she reaches behind her and rubs Eddington's balls to assure a spend. She need not encourages him overmuch. He is still eager to please and his prick responds mightily to the challenge. It thickens even as we watch it entering and exiting Erna's snatch. Again, just as he is about to spend, Erna dismounts. The sperm flows in a somewhat-diminished stream and Eddington's shaft begins to wilt. Not yet!

Nannette returns to the fray and grasps his tool. Now Eddington's eyes begin to fill with awareness of his situation. Nannette pumps his tool roughly. It stiffens by slow degrees, by now there is apparently some pain involved, for Eddington squirms and a look of discomfiture crosses his face. Nannette tugs him until she is able to cram his pole into her sopping cunt. The procedure repeats itself, only this time Eddington spurts only slightly.

By the fifth go-round Eddington is gasping and he begins to beg for a respite. There is none. The girls continue to fuck him silly—or *dry*, I should say. By the time he is mounted for the seventh ride there is nothing shooting from the tip of his swollen, reddened cock. The spasms cause him not-inconsiderable pain, as does the excruciatingly slow stiffening of his prick. One final time and we decide he has paid sufficiently for his indiscretions.

After Eddington's punishment has been seen to it is time for dinner. I have Erna join Nannette and me. Her status is unique and straddles the roles of servant and equal. Sir Albert and Percy are at the table also, but after some initial exchanging of amenities they are instructed to keep their eyes on their plates and eat silently. They are not to speak unless we address them first.

I inquire of Nannette, "You have had your share of adventures since arriving at Wellingham. I wonder if you have any anecdotes to relate pertaining to the times before your visit here." I am temporarily distracted by the arrival of the latest dish, set upon the table by the same fun-loving maid who so amused herself with Eddington's balls. "Excuse me Nannette." I then address the maid, "What might your name be? I like the look of you."

She curtsies and smiles. "Maureen, Miss."

"I want you to join Clara in the first-floor punishment room tonight. I understand that a certain clumsy servant has pruned one of the garden hedges incorrectly and it looks quite frightful. Perhaps we can improve the attention he pays to his duties with the strap upon his bare buttocks." Maureen is delighted. I turn again to Nannette.

She ponders a moment more. "Well, Nina, I have thought of one incident that you and Erna may well enjoy hearing of, though it is likely to be found rather tame when compared to both your adventures with the Gräfin."

Erna and I assure her that we are most eager to hear her story and so she begins. From time to time we are briefly diverted by the arrival of some new succulent trifle at our table.

"Two or three years past I was romanced by a fellow who was a headmaster at a public school in southern Scotland. This was of course before I met my dear, gallant Percival. Who, after meeting him, could ever love another?" We all laugh at this, causing poor Percy no slight discomfort.

Nannette continues, "The incidents in question occurred when I journeyed to visit my admirer at the school where he was employed. Indeed, I myself found a temporary position there as a governess for a small group of younger boys. My admirer and I took long walks in the countryside and dallied in flowered meadows. It was at one such romantic tryst that I first induced a male orgasm by gentle manipulation from my hand and have found it quite fascinating ever since." We all laugh at this, except for Percy who looks quite apoplectic. "Well, anyway, it was my admirer's duty to chastise the older boys on occasion when their behavior warranted it. One bright afternoon he invited me to be witness to such a punishment session. I disguised my eagerness to see such proceedings under pretended indifference. At last I 'reluctantly' agreed to be present when he caned an older boy for impertinence. You must understand I was actually thrilled at the prospect, for I knew the lads were caned while naked from the waist down. When the big moment came I was sitting in a comfortable seat just in front of my admirer who stood ready holding a cane, and with sleeves rolled up and waistcoat unbuttoned, ready to do his duty. I must confess that beforehand I had donned one of my best dresses and one of my finest hats. I also drew on my most expensive silk stockings and most stylish shoes. The lad entered and was quite surprised to see a female witness placed to view his punishment. I think the lad hoped that because I was present he would not have to remove all clothing from his lower half. He was soon disabused of this notion and forthwith stood 'bottomless' before us. My admirer, making no concessions for the lad's privacy, had him stand with his arms raised and fingers laced behind his head. I was so placed as to have a clear view of the lad's privates and in fact was quite taken with his large cock and fat balls. They were wreathed by a fine growth of hair that was just sprouting on his belly.

"The lad himself was deeply chagrined at this humiliating exposure, but the application of the cane to his bottom soon set his mind to more pertinent concerns. I must confess my admirer employed the strength of his upper arms to full advantage in the wielding of the instrument of correction. On and on the blows fell. The boy finally lost all semblance of stoicism and burst into tears. Throughout the proceedings I must reveal that I was fascinated at the way his balls bounced at every stroke of the cane. I rewarded my admirer most suitably in a romantic interlude but an hour later.

"I am somewhat ashamed to admit that the whole episode so excited me that I took my admirer's pole in my mouth and licked him up and down. I concentrated most heavily on the head, for my strokes there seemed to impart the most pleasure. But he was equally in my power when I slid my tongue along the entire shaft and even popped his balls one at a time into my mouth. He apparently could not withstand this treatment for long, for I felt his tool swell in my mouth as I pumped it and immediately thereafter he released a torrent of salty spermjuice that filled my cheeks as though they were balloons. I swallowed as much of it as I could and let the rest dribble past my lips. I'm horrified to say my admirer, upon seeing this, began to kiss my lips and lick up the remainder of his own spendings!" She paused for a moment, as if to compose herself, then continued.

I connived to be present during a second punishment session as well. This also involved an older boy, but the offense he was guilty of greatly struck my fancy. He was accused of stealing one of the governess's stockings and was actually caught masturbating with them. I was told he had the stocking wrapped around his balls and prick and with the feel of it close against his skin he was pumping himself frantically. My admirer laughed much when telling me of his punishment session. He would deal with this boy in my presence.

"The youth stood naked from the waist down, facing me, fingers laced behind his head. My admirer took up a light whip and began the correction. He striped the boy's buttocks nicely. I was sitting with my legs crossed. My skirts revealed my ankles and calves perhaps a bit more than modesty would dictate for such an occasion. I noticed the lad's eyes quite glued to my legs. Being then taken with a very mischievous idea I shifted position in such a way that my legs were exposed above my knees. It is quite possible he even had a glimpse of my muff…just as I intended. During a break in the lashing I complained of the heat and drew off my dainty shoes, exposing to the lad's fevered gaze my silk-stockinged feet. Of course my legs were still somewhat spread. I thought the poor boy would swoon at the sight. Randy schoolboys are quite starved for the sight of feminine charms and his eyes fairly popped from his head." We all laugh merrily at this and urge Nannette on with her tale.

"After the short adjournment to the proceedings my admirer took up the lash once more to continue the lad's corporal lesson. I put my feet up on a hassock near my seat, the better to give the hapless victim a full view. I rather took delight in arching my feet upon the hassock and wiggling my toes, all the while making sure that my skirts revealed me rather generously to the culprit's worshipful gaze. I was amused to note the swelling of the lad's cock proceed from minimal to full magnificence. My admirer, standing behind the boy and laying on the stripes, could not see the way that youthful shaft bobbed and bounced above the surprisingly large balls. I was quite enthralled at the way his body saluted my charms. I noted with amusement that his eyes were locked dreamily upon my barely-concealed pussy even when the whip was flaying his bottom most diligently. I was not, however, prepared for what came next.

"I was watching the lad with an amused smile upon my face at the spectacle he presented, when without warning I saw his prick begin to twitch rhythmically. The lad was now being driven to tiptoe by the force of the blows being applied to his posterior and he thrust his hips well forward. He didn't cry out or complain. Rather, his eyes became bleary and his mouth hung slack. Then, to my amazement, I saw the evidence of his excitement pour from him in thick stringing arcs to spatter the floor at my feet. My, but he was certainly plentiful! His sperm geysered out in great gouts that did not subside for nearly a minute. When he finished spending I played the coquette and told my admirer what had happened. He was quite disgusted and this led to further punishment for the boy. I was most flattered and pleased that I could stimulate a young rascal to orgasm just from the sight of my body."

Erna and I laugh and congratulate Nannette on her story. Sir Albert is properly downcast but trembles slightly. He has the vision of her tale. Dear Sir Albert! Perhaps he envisions himself young again and spurting upon the floor in tribute to a pretty female tormentor. Males amuse me for they are all naughty boys longing to be firmly taken in hand.

I shall not be outdone in tales of past naughtiness. I recall an incident that occurred at Schonring Castle just months ago. "It seems a carnival traveled about the regions of Bavaria. On exhibit with this traveling spectacle was a gentleman of thirty who was but twenty-two inches tall! He was not misshapen in any way and was of perfect proportions. Due to an unfortunate genetic defect he was born tiny to two quite normal-sized parents. He was handsome and possessed of his full mental faculties.

"During a hiatus of the carnival season he was invited by the Gräfin to visit Schonring. He assented readily and the Gräfin found him to be an amusing and well-read conversationalist, as did we all. However, the Gräfin had other motives than he first realized when she offered him her apparently generous invitation. He soon came to be treated as more of a pet than a guest. Before long there was no limit to the indignities to which he was subjected.

"The Gräfin's maids had fine sport with this miniature fellow and found it most amusing to take him up on their laps and fondle him. The Gräfin herself often took him up into her own lap and during one such occasion she stripped him of all his garments in front of the laughing women. He, of course, did his best to resist, but the strength of his tiny arms was no match for even the most diminutive maid. He was soon struggling weakly and naked upon the Gräfin's lap. She held both his wrists in one of her pretty ringed hands and began to stimulate his genitals with her free hand. She gently rubbed his tiny penis between her thumb and forefinger giving great care—I can assure you—not to hurt the fellow while subjecting him to the most intense penile manipulations."

"I must say that we were all quite taken with this fine sport and leaned forward to watch the masturbation with rapt attention. The little fellow begged, pleaded and threatened in an effort to make the Gräfin cease. All was to no avail. She stopped a moment only to apply salve to the tiny little prick to assure it would not be rubbed raw by the proceedings. Actually, she had a pretty young maid apply the salve which, you can be sure, only added to the little fellow's misery. I shall never forget as long as I live how we all laughed to see the tiny foreskin drawn slowly up and down the tiny prick by the Gräfin's gentle fingers. At last the inevitable happened and the little fellow sank down upon the knees of his captor and quite thrust himself into her working fingers. He was defeated and he knew it. A moment later we were treated to the sight of his sperm—and a good deal of it there was—splashing the Gräfin's short lace apron, which she had donned for the occasion.

"After this he was often treated the same way. I remember at least one occasion when I myself took him up into my lap and removed all the clothing from his lower half. Then I bounced him upon my knee causing his tiny, though swollen cock much friction against my thighs. I continued in this manner until he came and it ran all down my legs, much to the amusement of two maids I was entertaining with the exhibition.

"The Gräfin had to eventually limit the maids' unsupervised games with him. She caught them forcing the little fellow to lick their quims and bottomholes and bullying him in other unseemly ways. Though even after this ruling, he was still often subjected to rude indignities. The Gräfin would have the maids lead him into the drawing rooms where she entertained guests. A maid would lead him in naked and he would then dance for the amusement of her guests and be milked of his sperm for all to see."

I assure Nannette and Erna that the little fellow was most discreet when he left us to rejoin the carnival. To divulge the indignities to which he had been subjected would only shame him further and he had no desire for that.

It is Erna's turn to tell a story of past adventures and she begins excitedly. "At Schonring we would often have what was called 'execution day'. It took place whenever the Gräfin hired a new male servant and was intended as a sort of initiation for him into his new life of servitude. A scaffold was set up in the middle of one of Schonring's courtyards and the entire castle staff would be assembled beneath the blue sky as if on holiday. Several maids would assemble a throng and have it arranged on and around the steps of the scaffold. The servant would be quite naked for his entrance save for a loincloth. He would then be faced with the sobering sight of a great wheel in the center of the platform, and standing on each side of it, two pretty maids wearing hoods and elbow-length leather gloves. These grim vestments were in stark contrast to the maid's bare charms—for they were naked save for the hoods and gloves.

The unfortunate would then be fastened to the wheel with thongs and divested of his loincloth. Next he would find himself on the receiving end of a not-to-severe whipping, applied with relish by the grimly-costumed maids. When he was properly convinced of his own unworthiness and lack of manhood and after many pleadings and writhings under the lash, his tormentors would relent and cease. Then they would step forward and masturbate him to orgasm as the crowd in the courtyard cheered them on. The manipulations were very slow and drawn out, I can assure you, and the victims would soon be squirming and pleading for release as earnestly as they had begged before for an end to the whipping."

CHAPTER V

After dinner I summon Collette. She and I go to Eddington's room and enter. The poor fellow lies naked upon his stomach across his bed. His buttocks are covered with lines and welts. We sit beside him. I gently run my fingers through his hair.

"I fear by the look of your buttocks Nannette and Erna taught you a stern lesson, did they not?"

He nods. "Yes Miss."

"Did Clara urge them to be yet more severe with you?"

"Yes she did, Miss."

"Well, don't take it too hard, Eddington. You angered her when you came upon the carpet as she rode you. She was right to be angry at your impudence. However, it is in the past now and I have present concerns."

Collette and I help Eddington to his feet. As I had hoped, his organ is hugely swollen. I want it at my bottomhole. I take delight in the penetration of my anus by a soundly whipped and humbled servant. Collette and I stimulate Eddington to greater proportions still with our insolent fingers. His cock throbs in our warm hands. The helmet is enormous. A pearly drop glistens at the tip. His balls hang full and pliant between our fingers. I kneel upon his bed as he stands dumbly looking on. Collette lubricates my bum from a vial of lotion. She applies the rest to Eddington's rigid prick. She leads him by his prick to me and puts the head against my hole. She prods him and he pushes into me. The pain is excruciating only for a moment. Then she slaps his buttocks and he sinks into me. I am deeply penetrated by his girth. I have him grasp my hips and lift me up in his arms as his organ fairly splits me. He thrusts with groans of pleasure. I am skewered. I am lifted off my feet. My bare heels pummel his knees. My cheeks are hot coals. I gasp at how his rampaging tool fills me. Eddington goes up on tiptoe. He grunts and spends thickly while wiggling his hips and reaming me deeply. I gasp and mew in the liquid delirium of my own orgasm.

At last I feel his weapon slowly slide from my ass. With a plop it is out, but it still jerks against my buttocks and dribbles leftover come down the inside of my thigh. Collette is flushed. She has had her fingers in his bottom-hole. Eddington dares to kiss my neck. I shudder and spend again as his sperm seeps from me.

An hour later I am lying upon my bed. My mind is full of delicious dreams and plans for the morrow. After I set the events of the coming day in order within my mind, sleep takes me. As I sleep I dream that I am the lead dancer in a fine ballet troupe. I am naked beneath my short fluted skirt. My upper garment is of white lace and its sleeves taper into delicate gloves. Its long sleeves and high collar are in contrast to my bare bottom and cleft, which are revealed each time my skirt swirls up as I dance. My hair is up in a tight bun. My face is sweetly composed in an expression of almost haughty detachment and concentration.

Males dance with me. They are all swollen and in a state of great sexual excitement. This is plainly revealed as they are naked save for short-waisted shirts with padded velvet shoulders and long sleeves. I cause their swellings yet dance past them disdainful and unheeding. I swirl and pirouette, pointing my toes daintily on the polished marble of the dance floor. Beyond the footlights a veritable sea of faces watches my performance with rapt admiration. In the eyes of the men I see a longing to have me that is so great as to almost be a physical presence. In the eyes of the women there is admiration of the sort that is unmixed with jealousy. The greatest admiration is always unmixed with jealousy, as it is reserved for those who have attained an almost unmatchable superiority in some field or pursuit.

In accordance with the choreography of the dance I must now grasp the members of the male dancers as I swirl by. As I grasp each cock it begins to twitch and spurt. The spendings are thick and copious and they spill onto the polished floor like a tribute brought before a conqueror by vanquished multitudes.

In the center of the great dance floor now, a circle of naked male dancers lie upon their backs, legs spread. I dance to them flexing my legs and pointing my slipper-encased toes. I then step from one to the other carelessly using them as a sort of human bridge. As I tiptoe from one swollen prick to the next. I leave a trail of sperm behind me from those spouting spigots. I feel the cocks twitch beneath my feet. I savor the heat of them beneath my feet. Before they spend I am away and treading on the penises of those next in line. My feet are thus never soiled with the spendings my lightsome steps have provoked.

I dance next along the rear wall of the amphitheater. Fastened to it are more naked male dancers. As I dance by, I grasp their organs each in turn and they come.

At last as I swirl into the center of the dance floor once again—I see him. The lead male dancer. He, like the others, is naked below the waist. His tool is huge and hard and every female eye in the audience is glazed with longing. He grasps me by my curving hips and lifts me up. He holds me up high as he in turn spins about. My cleft nestles in his palm and I am wet. He then lifts me up before him and impales me from behind on his great swollen penis. My expression is still one of haughty imperiousness—even as I spend and spend again as he thrusts within me. Our parts gyrate locked together in full view of our admiring audience. His cock then slips from me and swells to Herculean proportions. I am now astride it, my legs locked straight, my toes pointed. My clit throbs hotly against his unhooded cockhead. He still supports me with his hands on my hips. I tighten my legs around him and he drives his branding iron against me and then deep into my pussy again. As we twirl he thrusts in and out to full length. I push up against him to suck his tool in more deeply and he responds by matching my motion. His balls slap my bottom with the intensity of his thrusts. I am lusciously impaled and I bob up and down on the pole that threatens to exit my mouth so deeply is it embedded. Suddenly he stiffens and his cock swells to immense proportions. He holds me away from him and pulls his tool from my gasping cunt. It beats against my belly as his sperm geysers from him in a pearly stream. Thick manhood spurts from him splashing the polished floor. Women in the audience watch raptly, lips parted, eyes wide with admiration. I awake to the sunshine laughing. I have kicked off my covers and lay naked upon the sheets.

The morning is full of preparations. I have planned an excellent diversion and accordingly have sent a carriage for Jane. To the rear of the house, alongside a sunny flowered embankment, is a smooth, flat field. It is surrounded by hedges and therefore is most private. We shall have a "pony" race. The carts are assembled and ready. How imaginative the Gräfin is when she sends gifts!

I have sent a note with the carriage to Jane. In it I suggest that it would be fine sport to trade Percy and Reginald. Percy would profit by the time spent under Jane's discipline. It would do him a world of good. Reginald would profit as well from a change of pace. Being tied down to a bed and teased by pretty maids is an excellent start to the training of a young male. But his training should proceed to other refinements of submission. Where better for this than at Wellingham?

My mind wanders back to the pony carts. They are an exquisite invention of one of the Gräfin's friends. They are small lawn vehicles designed to be drawn by naked males who are upon all fours, while a naked woman kneels in comfort upon a little velvet covered seat behind.

Jane, and hopefully Reginald, will not arrive until early afternoon. Nannette and I are in languid discussion in one of the drawing rooms when Clara informs us that we have a guest.

We receive our female guest in the comfort of the room wherein we have been conversing. We make our formal greetings. The lady is Elizabeth Wimley—one of Sir Albert's neighbors. She informs me that she has perused my advertisement concerning the training of young males. She has a nephew, age nineteen, who she feels would profit handsomely by such subjugation. She describes him as a handsome lad, well-rounded, save for the need to be taken firmly in hand and instructed by a member of the fair sex for a time.

I like Elizabeth Wimley. She and Nannette seem to enjoy one another's company as well. She has a bit of shyness about her, yet I feel that there is more beneath. I will now test her mettle. Under the pretence of touring the house and showing her about, we enter the downstairs punishment room. It appears to be just another drawing room of sumptuous comfort when all its equipage is stowed away.

Nannette has excused herself in order to attend to various household affairs. I have Collette bring tea for Elizabeth and me. As Collette's graceful hands pour tea into our cups from the silver pitcher, Elizabeth's eyes fall upon a large, upright wheeled box set in one corner of the room. It is one of the same type as the Gräfin used for the milking or punishing of male servants. I find them excellent for the same purposes. I have had this one set purposely in the downstairs punishment room. It contains a bound male servant—one of the lawn boys, I think. The opening from which his buttocks and genitals protrude is faced away from Elizabeth and me. Clearly she has no idea what the punishment box contains.

Her eyes question me.

"Oh, that is a tool for the disciplining of male servants. We find that after they have been placed within such a thing for a short time, helpless, upon their backs, legs drawn up, that they show much less impertinence for a long while after." I smile warmly at Elizabeth. "Such methods are unusual, I will grant you, but they are most effective and contribute greatly to a servant who is very efficient and most courteous."

Elizabeth nods slowly. "Are they not hot within the close confines of the box along with all their clothing?"

I smile again. "They have no need of clothing within the box, so they are deprived of it. They are quite naked. I am sure they are comfortable. You need not concern yourself Elizabeth."

I have myself called from the room briefly. I excuse myself and leave the room only to enter the small gallery which looks secretly back into the punishment room. Nannette awaits me there. We look through the peepholes and wait with bated breath. From where we sit we have clear view of the servant's genitals and buttocks. We whisper together. "She will explore the room but she will not touch him."

"Yes she will! She will touch his penis. She believes herself to be alone."

Elizabeth looks about. She is alone in the room. Her privacy is complete. She sets her teacup down gracefully, with its saucer, upon a small table. She purses her lips and rises. She strolls about the room, her gloved hands behind her. She moves nearer the punishment box. All the while her eyes linger on the fine paintings which adorn the walls of the room. She flicks a mote of dust from the gilt frame of one painting with her immaculate white-gloved fingertip.

At last she reaches the punishment box. She slowly walks around it. She flushes when she sees the servant's bare bottom and genitals exposed to her gaze. Nannette and I stifle our giggles. Elizabeth listens for sounds from the door. She hears none. She seems content that I will not soon return. She slips the white glove from her right hand. Her eyes are wide. Her cheeks flush a deeper red. She reaches down and tentatively touches the limp prick with her fingertip. She is surprised as the penis begins swelling almost immediately. She touches it again this time more boldly, though still with just her fingertip. The male inside believes that a maid has come to masturbate him. The maids often prolong the teasing before the milking begins. The male is swollen, for he knows his relief is imminent. Elizabeth is obviously quite taken with the helpless and swollen tool before her.

Now she grasps it in her fist. It nestles thick in her warm palm. The contrast is delightful. I love the contrast between a woman's dainty hand and a rude, swollen male organ. Elizabeth's lace sleeve hangs down upon the servant's balls. What a poignant picture this would make! Nannette and I are enthralled. Elizabeth squeezes the penis gently and then more firmly. It jumps and enlarges still more. A small bead of arousal drips from the engorged head. Elizabeth lets go of the penis and dabs at the moisture with her thumb, then licks the drop from her finger. She is smiling now. She has the enjoyment of slow, leisurely fingerings.

She grips the cock again and begins to work it in her little fist. The servant's balls slap against his bare bottom in time to her workings. She takes his large sac in her still-delicately-gloved left hand. She kneads the wrinkled skin of his sac to watch the fat plums slide about within it. She gently twists the scrotum and then weighs it upon her palm. How indecent it is! A man's balls dangled and teased upon a properly-clad woman's white-gloved palm. I shall wear gloves more often when I milk males. I love the picture it makes!

Elizabeth begins to work the throbbing pole in earnest now. The loose skin slides up and down the swollen tool, covering and then uncovering the darkening head. Elizabeth pauses for but a moment to withdraw a lace handkerchief from her reticule. She holds the handkerchief over the tip of the servant's penis with her left hand as she furiously flogs it with her right. Nannette and I can clearly see the cock twitch as she at last provokes his ejaculation. The handkerchief fills and rounds as it absorbs his effusions. Elizabeth drains him with an expression of slightly disdainful fascination upon her face. She then tucks the handkerchief away, composes herself, sits back in her place, draws on her right glove, and then picks up her teacup again to await me.

I soon rejoin Elizabeth and invite her to remain for lunch. She joins Nannette and me at the table and seems to enjoy herself—though not to the extent she did minutes before in the punishment room. Clara's eyes are knowing as she serves us. Perhaps she found it harder than usual to draw her punishment box victim to orgasm. I have no doubt, however, that she prevailed.

Elizabeth agrees to soon send her nephew, Robert Leighton, for my tutelage. I inform her that I shall be in London for a time. There are certain upcoming social events there that I do not wish to miss. I shall spend a few weeks at Charingate House. My uncle kindly placed it at my disposal. Elizabeth and I agree that I shall see to her nephew there. Nannette and I see her off. As her carriage sweeps down the drive another is waiting to enter. It is

Jane and, yes, Reginald also. He shall be placed under Erna's thumb while I am at Charingate. Erna will have him pliable in no time at all.

Jane and I embrace tenderly. I have indeed missed her very much. Reginald stands stiffly, hat in hand, his eyes upon Clara and Collette. He knows they, under Erna, will be his masters. I fear the lad may be developing a fear of maids. A bit of fear is fine as long as there is worshipfulness along with it.

It is a fine day with much warm sun. I see to it that Jane is given refreshment. Then we all retire to the hedged lawn for afternoon games. It is time for the pony races to begin!

Jane is in fine humor and truly looks lovely. She and Nannette have been visiting and have found much in common. Reginald has been given over to Erna's tender auspices for pony race preparation. Erna and Clara oversee the proceedings. There upon the grass in the sunshine Jane, Nannette and I doff all our clothing.

Jane's buttocks are full and promise the enjoyment of passion. Nannette is more lithe, yet still fulsome and curvaceous. The maids bring out the three males that shall be our ponies and draw our carts. Horst is swollen huge already. Pretty, red-headed Maureen leads him by a short leash and she is smiling and blushing. Collette leads Totworth and Clara leads Reginald. I think Clara has taken a liking to Reginald. She cannot resist tweaking his hard penis from time to time. This is great sport for her. I should not wonder if she has made him come already.

Jane, Nannette and I are all comfortable with our nakedness. It should be so. Women are to be served and pampered when they are naked. Males must see to the proper performance of their duties when they are naked. Naked women should be languid. Naked men should be dutiful and obedient. I chat with Nannette and Jane as we watch the maids prepare our "ponies." The carts consist of a small cushioned platform between two light wooden wheels. A wooden shaft rises curving from the front of the platform, tapering as it goes. At the end of the shaft is a crossbar.

Horst is brought on all fours to kneel under the shaft of Jane's cart. A thick leather belt hangs from the shaft and is buckled about his waist by Collette. Erna fastens the leather straps that hang from each end of the crossbar about his shoulders. Clara, Maureen and the other maids keep a watchful eye on Totworth and Reginald as the preparation of Jane's cart continues. Erna now instructs Collette in the proper fastening of the testicle leash about Horst's balls. The testicle leash—a thin length of ribbon that won't truly cause any injury—passes up through a ring in the shaft where it is looped. The woman who is borne by the ignominious pony can thus control him with a series of jerks upon his leash. We have found this method quite effective. Horst is at last fastened in place and Jane's cart is ready.

Preparations continue on the other carts and their beasts of burden. Totworth is soon secured to Nannette's cart and Reginald to mine. During this process the males show varying degrees of erection, especially when the testicle leashes are fastened about their balls. I am sure it is most humiliating to them to be treated thus. This is how it should be. In his degradation the male, at last, comes to realize his true place and is no longer an insufferable boor.

Now we three mount our carts. We all kneel, resting our bare buttocks upon our heels as this provides the optimum balance in accordance with the design of the carts. It also provides us with easy access to the testicle leashes which control our steeds. Every female on the entire Wellingham staff has turned out as if on holiday to enjoy the spectacle. The race will consist of three laps about the lawn. The winning pony will be masturbated by his rider and the losing pony will be birched by his. The second place pony will just be admonished to do better the next time.

All is still. I am flushed and ready. My hands firmly grip Reginald's testicle leash. Erna raises a pink ribbon, then lets it fall to the grass as a signal that the race has begun. Our ponies are off! Jane takes the early lead. She is a cruel rider and nearly castrates Horst in her excitement. She mercilessly jerks his testicle leash to inspire him to even greater efforts. The softness of the ribbon only seems to stimulate his cock to greater proportions. Totworth is but a neck ahead of Reginald. I smile at Nannette as we contest second place. We have nearly completed the first lap now and our ponies are in a fine sweat. They are truly exhausted for the wooden carts they draw have not been made with their comfort in mind. I tighten my legs and thrust out my hips. My cleft is wet with excitement.

Halfway through the second lap Jane's jerking of her mount's testicle leash proves her undoing. With a groan Horst throws back his head and spurts all over the grass to "Ohs" and "Ahs" from the watching maids. Jane's pretty face flushes in vexation and embarrassment. Nannette and I sweep past. We enter the last lap. The knees of the males are bruised now and their breath comes in short panting gasps. Jane has been left behind, though Horst is now trying for second place to avoid the cane. It is a contest between two of us now. Reginald and Totworth are neck and neck. To inspire Reginald to greater efforts I flick the leash to snap the back of his testicles. The ribbon is tight and he cries out and expends the extra effort. Reginald crosses the finish line a split second before Totworth! Horst comes in a quick third.

I roll off my cart onto the grass laughing and naked, there to be joined by Jane and Nannette. We embrace and laugh at our poor ponies. They are nearly fainting with exhaustion and their sides heave with each agonized breath. The maids at last unfasten them from the shafts of their carts. The time for reckoning has come. Horst is made to lie across the shaft of his cart and is held still by Clara and Maureen. Erna gives the birch to Jane. Jane accepts it, smiling, and then before all the gathered company she proceeds with the flaying of Horst's buttocks. She lays on energetically, up, down and across, and even undercuts from time to time so that the flexible tip of the whip nips at Horst's scrotum. She at last stops long after his buttocks are bruised and covered with dozens of parallel welts. She has given her arm much exercise in her private tawsing room. I am surprised Reginald did so well. I reward him. I have him down upon all fours. The maids gather about to watch. I kneel beside him and reach between his legs from behind to grasp his penis. I pull it back so it angles almost painfully and begin the stroking. I pump him up and down gently, then with greater force. His tool is rock-hard. The head is scarlet and burning hot. In moments he trembles. His sperm shoots thickly down upon the grass to the cheers and giggles of the watching maids.

The evening is spent in preparation for the trip to Charingate House. The trading of Reginald and Percy is finalized and meets with Jane's approval. When I inform her that Percy needs the most stringent discipline her eyes sparkle with relish. Erna shall manage at Wellingham most excellently. She has a gift for such things and is a natural wielder of authority. Collette and Maureen shall be her able assistants. I mean to take Clara with me. She is amusing in the way she enjoys the subjugation of males. She is audacious and imaginative with but a hint of impudence. I ask Nannette if she would like to accompany me to Charingate House as well. She is pleased and accepts my offer without a moment's hesitation. I have become most fond of her and value our talks and friendship.

Jane surprises me. She offers the services of Belinda. She tells me that Mary is most capable and, along with her parlor maid Ann, shall contrive excellent sport with the males. I accept the services of Belinda with gratitude. I still have the vision of Reginald licking her bottom as he is whipped with nettles. Her face flushed so prettily with the enjoyment of it. I embrace Jane and thank her most profusely. The servants I have installed heretofore at Charingate House are most discreet and capable, but lack the imagination necessary for inflicting dominance.

I shall return to Wellingham in a matter of a few weeks—two months at the outside. I instruct Erna most explicitly as to the milking of the males. Sir Albert and Eddington are to be seen to in a more gentle fashion than

Reginald, Totworth and Horst. I remind Erna that Sir Albert has a penchant for viewing bare female backsides as he is slowly drawn of his sperm. Erna giggles. She shall not forget. I can see it now. Sir Albert's big tool slowly teased in the warm hand of a willing maid while his fevered eyes linger on the curves of Erna's supple bottom. She will see to it admirably.

Jane and I visit late into the evening in the downstairs drawing room. We sip more fine old ruby port. She is full of ideas as to the proper running of her household and I listen to them all. I also am excited about Charingate and have many plans to implement. I shall enjoy the many social events that only a large city can provide. We talk until we are quite aglow with the effects of the port. We soon are embracing and we kiss each other gently upon the cheeks. I raise my skirts. I am naked beneath. Jane instructs me then like I am a schoolgirl and I play her little game.

"Nina, dear, please keep your dress raised and bend over to bare your bottom to me. I wish to inspect your parts to verify that you are chaste. I hope I shall find no salty effusions deposited by some wicked male!"

I giggle and comply. I am bent at the waist, my bottom is bare and thrust out saucily. "Oh my heavens! What a thing to say. I wouldn't hear of such a thing. Your exploring fingers shall find me perfectly untouched!"

Jane's fingers flutter about my cleft and boldly invade my foliage. My lips open willingly to her explorations and I am very wet. While one of her hands busies itself with the cupping of my mount the other spreads my bottomcheeks to find my anus. Gentle rubbings prepare me for Jane's probing finger. "You seem inviolate enough in front, Nina, but I must check behind as well. I am sure many a young man would love to be thrust in your bum up to his balls and panting like a randy bull. I daresay your innocent bottom would try diligently to expel the rude invader, and perhaps at last succeed. Yet you would undoubtedly be soiled in the process."

I laugh. I cannot help it. While I laugh Jane probes my bottomhole, digging her fingertips into the cavity past the ring of muscle that attempts to restrain her. I am impaled from both ends. Her fingers work at both my pussy and my bumhole. She teases my clit while violating me deeply from behind. I can feel the sensual vibrations beginning in my lower depths. When the two fingers in my cunt begin emulating those that are in my ass—exploring up to the knuckles and pressing against the membranous walls that separate my tunnels—I orgasm in great, shuddering waves. I spend copiously upon Jane's fingertips. Afterward Jane spends also to my slow, gentle, and most thorough fingerings.

CHAPTER VI

We are settled at Charingate House. It is situated in a pleasant part of London at the corner of Sutton and Bracecourt. Robert Leighton is due at any moment.

At last Nannette and I are notified that he has arrived. We accompany Belinda to the front door. Belinda opens it and there he stands before us. He is a slender lad, dressed as I requested of Elizabeth that he should be, in a smart school uniform. He wears black shoes and folded-down socks, white trousers, and a tailored short-waisted jacket. He clutches his cap in one hand and his one item of baggage in the other. I am impressed with the lad. Though he looks younger than his nineteen years, he carries himself with a certain graceful quietness. I see a very intelligent and expressive face framed by well-trimmed dark hair worn a bit longer in front.

It is important to establish the order of supremacy at the outset. I step forward and take his chin gently in hand. The hansom that brought him pulls away from the curb. Belinda shuts the door. I felt it better for him to come alone, for this way he would be more adaptable. His eyes calmly survey me with but a hint of apprehension as I still cup his chin in my gloved hand. It must be a great indignity for him to be turned over to strange women by his aunt for training. I search his eyes and find what I so enjoy. I keep my amusement to myself, yet I am pleased. The lad's eyes have widened. He is quite swept away with me. I see the beginnings of worship now in his face. What an amusement it is! What power females have over the male.

"Robert, I am glad you have come. I hope to be of some service to your Aunt Elizabeth. It seems she deems you immature and lacking the development and confidence necessary to assume your station in life. I fear she also finds you a bit strong-willed and selfish. Here at Charingate House you will learn otherwise, I am sure. Now young sir, what do you have to say for yourself."

He is nonplussed. His eyes move from me to Nannette. Belinda stands primly nearby in case she is needed. Nannette has assumed a stern and disdainful expression. I have known of men who love to be gently tickled to orgasm while their masturbatrix wears such an expression, and little else. Males truly fascinate me. I await poor Robert's reply.

"I am sure I shall do my best Ma'am. I shall not let you down and will apply myself most diligently."

I smile despite myself. The little beast is so enamored he is prattling. "Very well, Robert. Please follow Belinda upstairs to your room. She will show you where to put your things. Obey her implicitly. She is not a servant here. She is more than your equal. You will learn and experience things here that may seem strange to you. To instill such a change as your aunt desires in such a youth as yourself is not done without great effort and unusual measures. Do not be surprised at anything you see, experience, or may be instructed to do. The usual rules of conduct have no application in this house for the time being—at least not to someone in your place of submission. I expect instant obedience Robert and have the means to make you regret any recalcitrance you may show.'

He nods his understanding. Already he is in awe of Nannette and I. "Yes Ma'am." He follows Belinda up the stairs to the second floor.

As their footsteps fade, Nannette takes my hand and giggles. "Oh Nina, I like him. I rather think you advised him well of his proper place straightaway. He will be most amusing."

I laugh with Nannette. "I mean to pay the most detailed attention to him Nannette, and I mean for you to help me at every turn. We shall shape and polish him until he is able to properly serve the fair sex in every respect. We shall keep him in his chamber for a time. While he waits he will have time to feel more and more like the new boy at public school. As you know Nannette, such 'new boys' are most easily manipulated."

An hour later I send Clara to fetch Robert. She leads him across the upstairs hall from his room to a dressing room equipped with a bath. Nannette, Belinda and I soon join them there. Clara has stripped him as I instructed her. He is an interesting sight. His body is well made and carries a certain grace. His balls are quite fat and his tool shows promise of good size when erect, though now it is small from the humiliation of being naked before four women. His hands cup himself in front. His face is very red indeed and his head hangs a bit.

"Keep your hands away from yourself, Robert! We have seen the likes of your privates before I can assure you. You are not so well hung as to make us swoon with desire for you." This from Clara causes poor Robert much embarrassment as it was intended to do. He moves his hands away to reveal a slowly-stiffening organ.

Belinda has drawn his bath; the tub is full of well-soaped water and steaming hot. I order him into the tub. I tell him to scrub himself well. The four of us leave the room for a short time to change into clothes proper for assisting a bather. We all return to him totally naked save for short white aprons that do very little to conceal our mossy quims and bottoms. Our breasts hang full and pendulous before his gaze.

Poor Robert is most constricted at the sight of us! He looks but once, then turns his eyes to the wall and trembles slightly. He does not dare look at us. Neither does he wish to be rude and totally avoid resting his eyes upon us. He is in a dilemma as to the proper thing to do. It is quite amusing.

Nannette and I sit on dressing chairs. The maids kneel beside the tub and boldly begin bathing him.

"But I have already seen to this!" he pleads, eyes suddenly wide. We make no effort to preserve his pride or his dignity.

"One cannot trust a youth to correctly bathe himself. It must be done by ladies to assure it is done in a proper manner," Nannette purrs smugly.

Poor Robert! His humiliations have only just begun. Clara and Belinda are most thorough in his bathing. Nannette and I watch as they lift his cock and soap it carefully in their bare hands. Then Clara holds his tool—which is now swollen indeed—up out of the way as Belinda takes his balls gently in both her hands and washes him with gentle kneading motions. Robert is nearly beside himself and squirms to the entertainment of us all.

"Sit still or I shall have you birched across a maid's lap for your insolence." I pretend anger and get up from my seat to stand over him. His eyes desperately avoid falling upon my slit as it is revealed beneath the lacy hem of my apron. "You are making it difficult for the maids to do their duty with you." I order Robert to apologize to the maids for his wiggling. He does so. Then I have him kiss the hands of the maids to show that he is truly repentant. Nannette and I watch his compliance with amusement. Clara and Belinda giggle at the touch of his meek lips to their hands.

His bath is at last over. I have Clara shave him. She has great skill with the razor. The area of his privates is lathered and Belinda holds his penis out of the way as Clara shaves him. Nannette's eyes quite glaze as she watches his swollen organ loll between Belinda's thumb and forefinger. His foreskin is drawn back and the engorged head is so red as to be purple. Soon Clara's deft fingers fulfill their task and he is as smooth as an infant. One would almost think we had applied the gelding knife to his balls. He is so ashamed of his new baldness he doesn't know what to do or say. It is most amusing to watch his pretences crumble. Nannette is developing a taste for such diversions. The nuances that can be applied are endless.

I have Belinda sit on a dressing chair. I command him, "Robert, lie down across her lap. We are going to examine you. Do as you are told and lie still."

His organ bobs as he walks to Belinda's chair. Belinda smiles at his anguish. He lays across her lap supporting himself with his palms flat on the floor at her feet. Belinda's bare feet are prettily arched, her heels pressed firmly against the legs of her chair. I take a wooden phallus from a nearby cupboard and oil it slowly in front of Robert. Clara and Nannette smile. Belinda brings her legs together to imprison Robert's cock securely between them.

"No...please! Not that...No."

His pleas falls on deaf ears. One by one we all take

turns and insert our oiled fingers in Robert's tight bottom. At last he is stretched and prepared. Nannette grips the phallus and probes his ring with its tip.

Robert groans. The phallus slides into him deeply. Clara and Nannette take turns wiggling it about and cause him rather intense discomfort. We slowly tease and goad Robert beyond endurance. He wiggles his legs and gasps. He is trying not to come on Belinda's lap. We sabotage his efforts to contain his sperm. Belinda's thighs rub him. I reach down to hold his balls. Robert goes rigid. He clenches his jaw and his eyes widen as he spends profusely upon Belinda's lap. We have him up. A string of sperm glistens from his pintle to a white puddle on Belinda's apron. We all feign outrage. Clara spanks his bare bottom with her open hand until his cheeks are smarting. We tell him he was most rude to Belinda to soil her apron so lewdly. We make him kneel to kiss her bottom. She stands prettily on tiptoe, hands on hips, buttocks thrust out behind. Robert kneels upon the tiles and obediently kisses her globes. "Belinda, spread your bottomcheeks for him." She does, and we make him kiss her anus. He nuzzles it and licks heartily. Belinda has laughing eyes. Nannette and I watch another string of wetness dangle from his penis to the floor.

Nannette and I leave Robert in the charge of the maids with the most detailed instructions as to his tending. He is to go to bed very early and sleep in a nightshirt and nothing else. I tell Clara I want her to place a certain electric device upon his shaft. It is an invention of Dr. Hutton, given me by Jane. A wooden box with a dial and bell is connected to the penis by means of a cord. If Robert's cock stiffens the bell will ring, thus alerting the maids that he is being lewd with himself or having impure dreams.

Nannette and I prepare for a party to be held at a home on Argyll Street. I simply adore parties. One does miss them when one is in the country! Belinda assists us in dressing. I wear a black satin gown with a white embroidered front. It emphasizes the swelling of my breasts and bottom as I have planned it would. I draw on the most exquisite laced black gloves and my daintiest bowed shoes. My hat is of the latest fashion, small and sloped a bit downward in front with flowers and bows. A lace netting hangs over the upper part of my face.

"Oh it is simply beautiful. How it becomes you!" Belinda murmurs as she makes the final adjustments. Nannette smiles her agreement. She herself looks stunning in a creme and blue gown with a tight bodice. At last we are ready to leave. We have a carriage brought around front.

We sweep down the pleasant streets. It is good to be in the city again. One feels in the center of things in London or Paris. Nannette and I recline in comfort to watch the world go by our carriage window. We pass a hansom stopped to receive passengers. The driver helps a very pretty and haughty young woman up into the cab. My eyes drop below the driver's waistcoat. It is not my imagination! His organ tents his trousers in a salute to the woman he helps into his hansom. His eyes are fevered and locked on her briefly-exposed legs.

The party is a rousing success. The house is most elegant. It belongs to some stuffy personage or other who once was our ambassador to Sweden, or some such country. Geography has always bored me. One need only be the master of one's immediate surroundings to know fulfillment.

Nannette and I circulate about the rooms sipping a fine dry wine from Spain. Everywhere I look I see handsome men and regal women. Eyes are often upon me though I pretend I do not notice. When I am complimented I blush innocently and lower my eyes. Assumed innocence is often power when it comes to male propensities. Many males dream of having their organs gently pulled and goaded by a fascinated lady with wide, innocent eyes. They long to see her cheeks redden as her hand feels their hot spurtings.

In the midst of all this I am suddenly quite swept off my feet. I am introduced to the Viscount Charles Evelyn Highgate. What a fine figure of a man he is! He smiles at me and raises my gloved hand to kiss. As his lips brush my hand his eyes meet mine. I read bold and naked suggestions in his eyes. I blush and smile.

He steers me to a side drawing room where it is quieter. "How lovely you are! Do you know that you are truly a rare beauty. You have the look that drives men mad." His eyes drop to my cleavage and further down to the curve of my hips. "You are so proper with your hair up, yet I cannot help but think you are not as proper as you seem." He smiles.

His eyes are really rather adoring. I like it. "You seem to have no loss of words. Are you a poet as well as a Viscount?" I tease him gently. We talk a great deal and find we have much in common. He begs to see me again. In compliance with his persuasiveness I tell him where Charingate House is located. He wishes to come and pick me up late tomorrow afternoon. A picnic on the Strand is most improper, yet I laugh and accept.

Nannette and I converse all the way home. I feel a bit like Cinderella. Have I at last met my handsome prince? The Viscount is certainly most handsome. I laugh at the picturing of it. I am Cinderella. The Viscount kneels before me. His trousers are unbuttoned and his swollen cock is out. My skirts are high on my thighs. One of my silk-stockinged feet nestles in his gentle hand. The other wiggles naughtily in his lap gently tormenting his throbbing tool. At last he spurts between my toes.

When we arrive back at Charingate we sit in the library and relax a bit before bed. Clara and Belinda request a little of our time. They are most amused. They tell us of their games with poor Robert. Belinda is most loquacious.

"We had him in his nightshirt. The poor thing was so embarrassed he didn't know what to do with himself. We had him lie down upon his bed on his back and pulled up his nightshirt to place the masturbation alarm on his cock. He blushed so that we both couldn't help but laugh. Luckily he was a bit in shock from what we were doing to him so he didn't get hard straightaway. Clara held his penis still while I fastened on the wire. I think I may have made it a little too tight. We told him if we heard the bell it would mean he was being lascivious and there would be consequences. Then we left him. You tell the rest, Clara."

Clara continues. "The bell sounded three times all told. The nasty thing was as stiff as could be each time we checked him. We had him roll over and spanked him soundly with a hairbrush. After the second time his bottom was so sore we inserted the phallus in him and told him to see that he behaved himself. As you instructed, we were careful to tease and touch him whenever we checked the device. Belinda could not restrain herself and even gave him a few rubs, giggling the whole while!"

At lunch the next day we all present a rather strange tableau. Nannette and I sit at the table in nothing but tightly-laced whalebone corsets. Our breasts spill over the tops of them and our red nipples are luring to Robert's eyes. He is doubly discomfited because he is totally naked as he sits at the table beside Nannette. I sit across from them. The servants perform their duties as though nothing whatever is in any way unusual. Nannette's breasts are slightly smaller than mine, though with nipples rather more pronounced and pointed. Brave Robert! He avoids glancing at us for a very long time, but at last succumbs to the inevitable and darts slight glances at us. We appear not to notice his impropriety for quite some time and are instead addressing ourselves to a discussion of the latest fashion in shoes.

Thinking that he is not noticed in his peeking, he becomes a bit more bold, and thus careless. He starts, visibly shaken, as I abruptly address him. "Robert, your eyes are not upon your plate where they belong. You find Nannette and I so fascinating that I daresay you have even forgotten that your plate is on the table before you." The maids serving us hide their smirks from Robert as his eyes seek about the room as if for an answer to my embarrassing question. Nannette fixes him with an icy stare that she used with marked success more than once on potential suitors at the party we attended the previous night. "Robert, you can be so obvious at times that it simply sickens me." I raise my bare foot placing it upon the front of Robert's seat cushion across from me. I slide my foot forward pointing my toes until they encounter his penis. It is very stiff indeed and I fancy I can feel every beat of his pulse against my toes. He gasps audibly at the encounter of my foot upon his privates.

"Are you randy, Robert dear?" I enquire most sweetly. "Poor boy, your peppermint stick appears to be all swollen. I do hope nothing is amiss." I gently urge and prod his penis now with my impudent toes. His face is really quite a picture! Nannette and I cannot help but laugh at the sight of it. We are really both soon overcome with amusement as I continue my lewd wigglings in his lap. Soon of course he is undone. He can no longer hold out. He begs for the unbearable stimulation to end. "No...Please don't. I mustn't...Oh, but it is going to happen anyway now. No!"

Nannette's eyes meet mine, then her gaze shifts back to Robert's lap. She is holding the tablecloth aside to watch him come. I continue the game. At last it happens. I feel Robert's penis twitch and push my foot against him yet more till I can feel his balls beneath my heel. I feel his hot flood squirt down over my toes as I watch his hands tremble against the pristine backdrop of the white tablecloth. Of course such indulgence on his part cannot be tolerated. I have Clara clean him and Belinda fetch a hairbrush. I then have him lie across my lap. Nannette spanks him soundly while he is in this position. His penis stiffens again as it is clamped tight between my thighs. I feel it nudge the thatch of my mount and spend myself—an exquisite sensation, though my face remains set in an expression of disciplinary disdain.

In the afternoon Charles picks me up in a closed carriage. He is ever the gracious gentleman. We discuss the theatre a bit and then grow bored with that topic. At last Charles seems to have made up his mind about something. He undoes his trouser buttons and withdraws his weapon. It is certainly of admirable proportions and rampant as can be.

"Nina, please put your hand upon it."

"I will not! I have never done such a thing!" My cheeks redden, yet my eyes feast on the girth and readiness of his tool.

Again I decline his lewd offer though my eyes caress his

prick. Charles looks so eager and his tool is fine indeed. It is long and thick and lightly veined. The head is a wonder of velvety dark flesh. I waver a bit. He beseeches me. I relent. I place my gloved hand in his lap and take hold of him.

"Yes, Nina, that's it. Please stroke it now in your hand. Just work it up and down a bit if you please."

I do please. My fingers pull his foreskin up and down his tool. I feel it straining in my hand. Charles sighs and rolls his eyes with pleasure. He then surprises me by placing his hand on mine to stop the frigging. His eyes beg me with more imploring than before. At first I do not understand. Then it dawns on me. He wants my mouth! At first I am angry, then I think for a moment.

I have rarely done such a thing as suck a man's tool and none could cajole me into doing so against my will. A lesser man I would have laughed scornfully at, slapped, and left swollen with longing. Yet, I have this delightful picture in my mind now. A closed carriage rolling through London and the woman inside sucking a Viscount's cock. How picturesque! I decide to drain Charles and suck him until he is weak. I bend over and take his prick in my mouth. His eyes widen in surprise. I took so long to decide that his eyes had already begun to show keen disappointment. His cockhead is as smooth as velvet. I swirl my tongue about it paying special attention to its sensitive underside. I keep his foreskin well drawn back and out of the way in my gloved fist. Charles has seized the arm of his seat. His knuckles are white as can be. I would laugh at him but my mouth is otherwise occupied at present.

The heat from his tool warms my mouth. I imagine his view as my head bobs up and down. He can see my hat and my hair up properly in back. I milk him with my fist and suck on him with greater vigor. I have a sudden urge to taste his sperm, to devour his manhood. I am licking his swollen head when he groans and I feel the first salty spurts upon my busy tongue. I take him in deeply and suck his spendings from him. I swallow almost greedily as my fist flies up and down his weapon coaxing a last spurt of his strength into my suckling mouth. At last I am finished with him. I sit up and set myself in order. I pat my hair to see that all is in place. I am a most proper woman again. A most proper woman with burning cheeks. I then look over at Charles. He is still sagging in his seat. His cock is still out of his trousers, though now it leans feebly to one side, softening as I watch. I meet his look of awe with a conceited gaze. Then I lick my lips and turn to look out the window. Passersby see an elegant carriage with a proper and pretty lady languidly surveying them from within. Which of them could ever imagine she has the taste of sperm upon her tongue?

Our carriage turns up the Strand. High in the distance are the towers of Westminster. The Thames rolls by unperturbed on our right. There are beautiful flower gardens, walks and pools on our left—most suitable for a picnic. Charles has the carriage stop. He gets the basket and we set out down a wide flagged path. We pass other strollers and others setting up their picnics on the grass. After about five minutes we arrive at a sloping lawn as smooth as glass beside a marble-rimmed pool. Here we set our things upon the grass in the brilliant sunshine. There are others about but none too close by. We talk and enjoy cold game hen and a crisp white wine from the Rhine.

After we have finished our lunch I soon find an excuse to bathe my bare feet and legs in the nearby pool. I wear a powder blue sleeved dress with a matching hat, and gloves. I tuck up my skirts and step down across the marble rim of the pool into the water. Charles comes further down the bank to sit on the grass nearby and watch me cool myself. I amuse myself laughing, splashing and high-stepping like a child. I kick water at Charles and giggle, for I have drenched his trousers. I am nearly ready to come out of the water when I notice that I am attracting more than a little male attention. Their eyes upon my legs are first appraising and then enamored. I continue my sport now, contriving to raise my skirts a bit more and wiggle my hips and bottom in my prancings. Two young men in school blazers are sitting by the water eyeing me hungrily. I am most gratified to notice that their trousers cover fat bulges between their legs. They stare while trying not to appear interested. They look at my thighs and legs and feet as though they would commit to memory every detail. I can imagine them tonight in their stuffy rooms in some college stroking their swollen cocks and thinking of my thighs until their milk spurts. I hope I giggle mockingly in their dreams as they helplessly spend.

On the coach ride back to Charingate, Charles and I have more amusements. "Nina I would like to see your bare bottom."

I act surprised, but, I willingly expose my charms by lifting my skirts well up above my hips. I bend over and present my bottomcheeks for his inspection. He rubs my buttocks then reaches under and slides his fingers into my nest. I am wet. His fingers are knowing and expert in their caresses. He fingers me in and out, burying them to the knuckles, probing, stretching, massaging. Charles then undoes his trouser buttons and slides them down to his knees. I smile at him and wiggle my buttocks.

"Would you like me to sit on your lap, Charles?" I inquire invitingly.

He gasps his agreement with the excellence of my idea. I lower my buttocks down upon him. He holds his tool and steers it to my anal opening. I adore the feel of a warm tool probing my bottom then sliding ever deeper into me. Poor Charles! He is so swollen I feel his throbbing entry into my fundament most lusciously. I gasp at the fullness of the penetration. How I love being impaled upon a stiff penis! I begin to milk him by working my anus upon his tool. It clenches and loosens, determined to draw his sperm from him. I will relieve him with my bottom. I will make him spend in my bottomhole. I flex my legs to raise and lower myself upon him. I go up on tiptoe so he almost escapes my bum altogether. I go down again and he is recaptured. He will not escape me until he has poured out his tribute of surrender.

"Oh, Nina, you are so very tight. I cannot last, I shall spend! I am spending!"

His voice tapers away to a moan and I feel his organ flex and jump. Then I am flooded with a sensation of warmth and even greater fullness as, in his ecstasy, he thrusts yet deeper. His fingers reach across my thigh and knead my clit. I orgasm suddenly, salting his hand most generously with my tribute. Charles sags back in his seat, drained, as the carriage rolls on. I have the self-satisfied smile of a cat as I again set myself in order. When we arrive back at Charingate, Charles is most sentimental. He kisses my gloved hand.

"Nina, you are a delight. You drive me mad. I must see you again very soon."

"Oh, Charles you really are a dear. I am sure I will see you again. I enjoyed our picnic very much. You are quite the gentleman." He escorts me to the door. A quick kiss upon his cheek and I am gone. I love the longing I see in his eyes. He is rather handsome and dashing. He carries himself with the confidence and assurance that the wealthy and established possess, though he is easily undone in my presence.

A day later Nannette and I take Robert for a carriage ride. I mean to increase the humiliation to which I am subjecting him. Well-applied comportment training for males is nothing at all if it lacks generous doses of humiliation. We have him bottomless in the closed carriage.

"Robert, I want you to stroke yourself for a bit. Take care that you do not spend, for if you do you will be birched, then caned on top of that when we return to Charingate." He is so meek! He takes my warning very seriously, but obeys and begins stroking himself. Nannette and I watch with amused smiles. Soon he has a fine erection. "Robert is it pleasurable when you stroke yourself?"

"Yes, Miss."

Nannette interrogates him further. "Is it pleasurable to stroke yourself while being watched by two ladies in a closed carriage?"

He blushes and hangs his head, but obediently keeps stroking. "Yes, Miss."

"Why is it pleasurable to stroke your organ in front of two ladies?"

"I don't know, Miss."

"Come now, Robert, there are reasons for everything. I insist you tell us the truth or it will be the worse for you. Why is it pleasurable in front of ladies?" He tries his best to answer but dissolves in helpless stuttering. We both laugh at his discomfiture.

I turn my attention to the carriage window for a moment. I signal the driver to pull up to the curbing where two pretty young ladies stand talking together. They have the look I am searching for. Two pretty, yet very spoiled privileged girls whose greatest problem is boredom. They have innocent, dimpled, cruel eyes. They are most suitable. I draw down my window and motion for them to come closer. I pretend to ask them directions to an obscure bookshop specializing in moral platitudes. Of course they notice Robert. He stopped his masturbating when they drew near.

"Robert, keep stroking! I have not told you to stop."

Both girls are now most interested indeed, and are fairly pop-eyed at the sight of Robert as he again begins stroking his swollen tool. One turns to the other and can hardly contain her glee.

"Look, Julia! He is masturbating!"

Nannette offers her calm explanation of the scene. "Yes, Robert has such a habit that we thought to make him do it in public, and thus shame him out of it."

Both girls are now on tiptoe outside the carriage window shading their eyes from the sun to see every detail of what goes on within. I invite them in and they most willingly accept, crowding into the carriage with us. Robert's foreskin is drawn well back and he has himself in hand frigging briskly as I have so commanded. He is so utterly nonplussed at having an audience of four pretty females that his eyes are totally stunned, almost as if he believes himself to be having an erotic dream

"May we masturbate him a little?" This from the girl whom her companion addressed as Julia. I say that they are most welcome to handle him for a bit and tell Robert to take his hands away from himself. He is in an agony of humiliation at present and his eyes beg me to refuse the girl's lewd request. They begin to avidly grasp and toy with him maintaining all the while their expressions of almost innocent wide-eyed interest. Julia amuses herself by pumping his tool up and down in her gloved hand while her companion is entertained by dandling his shaven balls upon her palm. Nannette and I are smiling our encouragement to the girls to continue their toyings and they do not disappoint us. Poor Robert has wetted Julia's hand a bit with the proof of his arousal. This further fascinates the girls who work him more vigorously. "Can we make him spurt? Julia has never seen a young man spill his sperm before." This from the dark-eyed companion of Julia who has removed her gloves to savor the feel of Robert's penis throbbing hotly in her bare hand.

"It is up to Robert. He knows that if he comes he will be soundly birched, then caned. This is to associate in his mind pain as being a consequence of onanistic indulgences. It is Robert's decision. He knows that his bare bottom shall pay for every spurting twitch. It may well be worth it to him. You have worked him nearly frantic by now. It would amuse us to see it."

Julia's companion leans forward to look Robert full in the face. "Shall we make you spend?" Her fingers continue his slow genital torment. "Wouldn't this delight be worth a bit of pain?" She asks sweetly.

Robert is in an agony of indecision. He desperately wants the pleasurable manipulations the charming girls so willingly give him to last forever. At the same time he knows that they will soon have him spurting. He is well acquainted with the pain of canings and birchings! The girls stop for a moment. He cannot bare it. "Oh. No, I... Yes! Please don't stop!"

His new friends are most eager to make him spend. They both are bare-handed now and work him shamelessly. Of course the outcome is unavoidable. His penis twitches and he knows it is too late, yet even in his pleasure the thoughts of his certain punishment torment him.

"No! Please don't. No! Stop! No!"

Nannette and I feast our eyes upon his spurting. His sperm arcs from his penis in thick floods to bathe the hands of his tormentors in warm effusions. His eyes twitch shut as the sensation masters him while the girls emit peals of laughter and try to catch his foaming jets in their hands. When it is over we help Julia and her companion clean their soiled hands. They thank Nannette and me profusely. Julia bends down and kisses Robert's cheek gently.

"We had fun frigging you. Now you shall have the birch and cane!"

At Charingate it is time for retribution. We will punish him in Nannette's dressing room. I have selected suitable attire for us. The disciplinarian must always be properly clad. Belinda assists Nannette and me in dressing. We don skin-tight white breeches, tucked into gleaming, knee-high, black boots. We also wear short-waisted black jackets, embroidered in blue by an excellent Spanish tailor. Our costumes are completed with the addition of black gloves and low-crowned Spanish hats. Of course we have our hair done up in the most severe buns.

We smile at each other then assume serious expressions when we hear Clara's knock at our door. Belinda opens it to admit Clara who leads Robert in by his cock. There is no time for him to beg. The maids have him down across a low dressing table. Belinda holds his ankles and Clara keeps firm purchase upon his wrists. Robert's fevered eyes watch Nannette's gleaming boots cross in front of him as she withdraws the birch and the cane from a nearby walnut cupboard.

Nannette smiles prettily as she takes up the birch and begins the application of Robert's correction. I stand nearby ready for my turn with the cane. It is truly a delicious pleasure to chastise a male. How helpless and silly they are! I daresay they deserve nothing better. The birch crashes across his bare bottom with great force governed by a skillful and measured rhythm. Robert tries to be brave but the pain he is being subjected to by an amused and most attractive lady unmans him. I am eager for my chance to show my skill. Nannette finishes thrashing him soundly with a series of strokes that find the crack between his buttocks. As his birching ends I begin. I take my time about it. I stand first on one side of him then the other. I paddle him well, though I refrain from putting all of my energy into it. I wouldn't want to damage the boy, especially not those manly balls and that hefty cock that have given us so much enjoyment. When I am finished he is sobbing. His bottom is latticed with an excellent diamond pattern of stripes. It is my most precise yet! Nannette hugs me and congratulates me as the maids lead poor Robert from the room.

CHAPTER VII

In the following days Charles and I see a great deal of each other. He tells me of his niece, Edwina, a pretty girl of eighteen who is found by her parents to be unmanageable. I quickly suggest she spend some time at Charingate with me. I say the change will do her good.

A day later Edwina arrives. Nannette and I both take to her at once. I have a long conversation with her. I inform her that females are by nature more spirited and willful and that this is a good thing. I tell her that those who have tried to harness her will are doomed to failure beforehand. She, like me, is a woman born to dominate and have her every whim catered to in the most satisfactory fashion. It only follows then that I see to it that Edwina and Robert meet. I have told her a little about him, but decide to let her see the true picture at an afternoon session.

Edwina, Nannette and I are comfortably situated in the drawing room. We await the bringing of our tea. No maid shall serve us today, however. We will have more entertaining diversions to occupy us. Edwina well knows something unusual is afoot. Her eyes flash with excitement, though she takes her cue from Nannette and me and remains properly reserved. I have given Robert the most careful instructions combined with the severest threats if he is careless of the smallest detail. I am not disappointed. There is a knock at the drawing room door and in he comes carrying the tea service. Edwina can hardly believe her eyes. Robert is naked save for a white lace apron tied about his front! It is a brief affair. One can just see the curve of the bottom of his balls hanging below the hem. Edwina looks from me to Nannette and then cannot help herself. She bursts into laughter at the sight of him.

Robert jumps and very nearly drops the tray. I have no patience whatever with him.

"Robert, your buttocks will pay well for your clumsiness if you mishandle that tray! See that you take care." He comes closer and sets the tea service down on a table near our chairs. Edwina stifles the last of her mirth and stares at Robert. I admire her eyes. Her gaze meets and holds Robert's. The amusement in her eyes holds him helplessly the way the pins hold a butterfly on the mounting board. Robert's eyes drop to the floor. I smile at Nannette and she nods. We have both noticed how Edwina masters Robert.

Nannette commands him, "Robert, you will serve Edwina first and you will do so with all the politeness you can muster."

Robert's acknowledgement is most mild. "Yes, Ma'am." He hands Edwina a dainty porcelain cup from the tray. She takes it, and then he pours the tea. His hand is shaking noticeably. Edwina is a fetching young lady and Robert is in an agony of embarrassment at being so naked before her. Her only thanks to him is a mocking smile. He turns from her to serve Nannette next. Alas, he remembers too late that his bottom still bares the marks of his most recent discipline. Edwina sees them and giggles. How precocious she is! Robert turns halfway to the side so his shame will not be presented to Edwina's view. This brings laughter from all three of us.

After Robert serves us he stands patiently by at our beck and call. When we have finished, his humiliation is increased. "Robert, present yourself to Edwina and raise your apron so she may see your cock and balls. I would have her inspect you a bit." He obeys as a condemned man who walks to the scaffold where hangs the rope. Edwina is enjoying every moment of his torment to the fullest.

He stops before her and raises his apron with an unsteady hand. Edwina leans forward to get a good look at him. For some reason the bored and somewhat petulant expression she has assumed takes his fancy. His prick begins to slowly lengthen and thicken before her very eyes. She watches this process to its completion with an expression somewhere between fascination and disgust. When he is fully hardened she reaches down and takes a napkin from beside her saucer. She grasps his penis with it and firmly draws back his foreskin. By instinct this girl knows just how to carry herself and what to say. She falls into the dominant role by some gift of natural ability. Nannette and I are both amazed by the speed of her progress. Edwina addresses us while still holding Robert's penis, with its foreskin drawn back.

"I suppose he is adequate, though one cannot help but notice he lacks a bit in girth. You have him shaved—that is most excellent. I do think it becomes him somehow." She weighs his balls in her palm. "Perhaps he lacks a bit of vigor here. I feel his balls are a trifle light." With a toss of her head she releases her purchase on his privates and I command him to drop the apron once again. I tell him to gather up the tea things and take them away. He is to return immediately.

When he is back we are ready for more games with him. Edwina sits with her skirts drawn up to reveal her pretty legs even to her stocking tops. Her garters are decorated with tiny lace roses. Her stockings are of the finest beige-colored silk. Her shoes have a large flowered bow on the toes and rather high heels. Her feet rest upon a velvet cushioned footstool. Robert's eyes do not in any way neglect her charms. I have given Nannette the pleasure of conducting this symphony of humiliation.

"Robert, you will now remove your apron," Nannette commands him. He does so and then she makes him kneel at Edwina's feet. "Now you will take hold of your cock and rub it until it is stiff. See that you stop as soon as it has achieved full hardness." Edwina watches intently as Robert obeys this latest instruction from Nannette. I am really rather fond of Robert and so is Nannette. I simply adore the purple of his swollen cockhead as it protrudes from his sliding fist. The poor boy is really quite overexcited. I have not allowed Clara and Belinda to masturbate him for several days past. They miss the indignities I allow them to subject him to. Their hands must crave the warmth of his spurtings. He is now stiff and stops his frigging.

Nannette continues her role of ringmaster in our little circus of amusements. "Robert, when Edwina raises her foot you are to place your cock between the heel and arched instep of her shoe. Then you are to work your hips to and fro." What a spectacle this presents! His penis is soon nestled beneath the arch of Edwina's little shoe, trapped between the instep sole and the front of the heel. He works himself back and forth thrusting in and out almost as if he is making love to her foot. Edwina looks down across her pretty knee at him. The pretty girl's eyes are almost tender. She has the desire to see him ejaculate. What a contrast it is—his swollen organ imprisoned by her dainty white shoe. "Stop, Robert. Hold very still. Edwina will now give you the soothing relief you crave." Edwina slides and wiggles her foot to and fro thus masturbating Robert with her shoe. His prick is quite chafed where her heel rubs him. At last she vanquishes him. He trembles, his cockhead grows enormous and he spurts upon the carpet. Edwina smiles and watches her shoe work back and forth, pulling his foreskin with it to coax and goad more spurts from him.

Of course, he must now be punished for his impropriety. Edwina knows and relishes her role in this as well. He is made to remain kneeling and rest his now-somewhat-softened penis on the velvet footstool. Edwina stands above him. She raises her leg to place the sole of her foot, bare now, flat upon his tool. She smiles and shifts her weight forward a bit, pressing his cock between the footstool and the sole of her foot. Robert must keep his hands folded behind his buttocks as this process continues. Edwina varies the pressure to which she subjects his penis. Sometimes it is very light—almost a caress. Other times she bares well down upon him, fairly grinding his lance into the velvet cushion of the footstool. With her bare foot the pressure she exerts is more pleasurable than painful.

Periodically she raises her leg and brings her foot to his lips. Then Robert must cover it with servile kisses and lick about the toe until they are shiny wet. Then her foot descends again to apply pressure to his most intimate parts. Despite having so recently spent and despite the mild pain the charming girl so willingly inflicts upon him, Robert's penis is again swollen with the urge to shame itself.

Edwina would go on for hours, I think, but we ask her to relieve him. She lightly rolls his penis beneath her arched toes and the velvet cushion of the footstool. Edwina wears a self-satisfied smirk as she feels the twitching of his penile surrender beneath her pretty foot. We watch his spurts arc down upon the floor.

In the evening Nannette and I travel to a party. Charles has sent a carriage for us. I am terribly bored at the party and Nannette is as well. Charles has been accosted by an acquaintance and excuses himself temporarily from our company. Nannette and I wander through the rooms seeking amusement. Males hover about us like a cloud of annoying insects. At last we find sanctuary in a small parlor. Its doorway is almost hidden behind the great curving staircase leading upward to the third floor of the house. There is only one other person within—a wallflower obviously. He rises eagerly to his feet upon our entry. His self-imposed exile due to lack of social graces has been terminated by the arrival of two pretty women. He plays the gracious host, though he is a guest like ourselves. He points out the painting on the wall and pretends some expertise in the arts. Nannette and I try hard not to laugh at him. Nannette stands between him and the door. I move close to him and rub my hand down the front of his trousers. He is so helpless I giggle.

I undo his trouser buttons and pull out his rather thin prick before he can collect himself or deny me. Quite casually, I begin to pump it up and down. His eyes move from me to Nannette like a startled bird. Nannette smirks at him then licks her lips. My hand works him briskly. His cock is small but at least it is an idle amusement for me to toy with him.

We hear voices in the hall. He is on the verge of panic but my hand will not allow him escape. I see the signs of his impending crisis. I lead him forward a bit while working his tool. I point it at the striped satin cushion of an elegant French settee. He is glassy-eyed as my hand milks his spurts down upon the cushion. His sperm erupts in three great gouts and slides down the back cushion to collect in a thick pool upon the seat. Abruptly we leave him with his dripping penis still out. The men we pass as we exit the room stroke us with their eyes. We blush as is proper at the affront.

After breakfast the next morning Robert's training commences once again. The maids have strapped him down to a punishment bench specially set up in the upstairs parlor. He lies naked upon his belly. His wrists are fastened together beneath the bench and his legs are secured to the legs. A thick leather strap passes about his waist to further immobilize him. His genitals and buttocks extend a bit back over the end of the bench so his disciplinarians have ready access to them.

Edwina joins Nannette and me. We instruct Edwina in the art of birching. We patiently teach her the finer points of this delightful skill. In her learning the dutiful girl wears out six birch rods on Robert's bare bottom. She is most conscientious in her quest for expertise. She wields the birch with the full strength of her arm, crashing the strokes upon Robert's buttocks in a pattern that is most pleasing to the eye. The welts cross each other in a pattern that resembles the weave of a fine material. The skin of the boy's bottom is swollen and terribly enflamed, yet Edwina continues without hesitation. She experiments with several techniques, simply flicking her wrist at times so that the tip of the birch licks at the taut skin, and raising her entire arm at others to bring the whip thundering down with dreadful impact. However, she seems to most enjoy using an undercutting motion that allows her to reach between Robert's buttocks and tickle his balls. Halfway through the proceedings it becomes necessary to gag Robert with a pair of Belinda's undergarments. Edwina is rather outraged by his lack of manhood under the pain of the birch and tells him to hold his tongue and stop acting like a baby. Nannette and I laugh at Robert's discomfiture.

Edwina—upon completion of her disciplinary duties—asks us if she might make him come. It is a most excellent humiliation for a male to be made to ejaculate by the very hands that punished him. Nannette and I consent.

Edwina asks for a bit of oil and we have Clara bring some in a small jade jar. Edwina oils the forefinger and middle finger of her right hand. Then while Nannette and

I watch, she thrusts her fingers into Robert's bottomhole quite up to the knuckle. She twirls and wiggles her fingers about rather roughly within him. It is obvious she has done this before.

"Edwina, where have you learned this skill?" I enquire of her amusedly. Nannette has moved forward to watch. She is fascinated. Edwina smiles and answers my question while continuing the lewd work of her fingers deep in Robert's bottomhole.

"During the summer past, my cousin Susan and I found the farm boy who lived in a cottage below our home to be fine sport. He was a simple rustic lad without culture or education. It amused us to listen to him talk and when we giggled at his homespun accent, he thought us to be quite taken with him. Rather we were using him as a clown to amuse us with his bumbling ways and speech. He was very enamored of us and, in his own ignorant way, was loyal and trusting. I fear we took more than a little advantage of the boy, though certainly, he never realized to what extent."

Edwina keeps her fingers probing deeply within Robert's bottom. He stifles groans of pleasure and discomfort. He tenses on Edwina's fingers trying in vain to expel their humiliating invasion of his person. Edwina giggles and continues her tale while Nannette and I watch her fingering proceed.

"One lazy afternoon, we had the farm boy enter a small copse of trees with us. We soon teased him into stripping there before us. He was more than a little proud of his enormous tool and was very disappointed when we blushingly refused to handle it. It was long and thick and possessed of a pair of balls as large as lemons! Certainly, we declared, we would never touch such a naughty thing. Susan shook her hair from her eyes and giggled. She whispered to me that she knew of a game we could play with him that she had seen her mother play with the gardener. We had the boy lay on his back naked and we knelt beside him. We commanded him to raise his knees up to his chest and promised if he obeyed us we would certainly delight him. I had no idea what Susan was up to at this point. She always knew more than I of such things."

Poor Robert's organ is now most turgid. He wets himself regularly with milky beads of arousal. Edwina's fingers are rude and shameless invaders as they give him no rest. He squirms in vain against his bonds. His buttocks are welted and covered with weals where Edwina's birch danced upon him. "Susan had me lift the farm boy's balls up out of the way. I was disgusted at the thought of actually touching them, so I just took a pinch of his skin between my thumb and forefinger and lifted them up. Susan laughed and said I had my little finger raised as though I were sipping tea at a lawn party. Susan then inserted her forefinger into the farm boy's bottom. There was no lubrication such as I have with Robert here. I think it hurt the boy a bit, but he lay there upon his back, knees drawn up, and let her insert her finger to the knuckle. I was more than a little fascinated with the proceedings and watched as Susan did to the farm boy what I am doing to Robert now."

Robert is quite beside himself by now and his eyes are so imploring I walk forward to stand by his head. I have him gently kiss my fingers one at a time. All the while Edwina's fingers thrust and wiggle within him and stretch his poor bumhole. Nannette strokes his cheek and smiles fondly down at him. Edwina goes on.

"As Susan's finger worked him, the farm boy muttered things that made us both laugh at him. He said that he wished he was firmly planted in our cunts up to the balls and was sure we would be most grateful for the good fun he could give us. In reality of course, the boy was on his back being degraded most completely by two young ladies who considered him little more than a dim-witted animal. His cock began to twitch and Susan told me to watch as he would soon be spending. I let go of his balls and let them fall back against Susan's fingers. Then I saw a male come for the first time. He went as rigid as a piece of iron and his prick fairly began bouncing against his belly. Then, as Susan and I watched, giggling, his sperm poured from him in a thick white stream to soil his own person—much to our entertainment."

Robert has come to the end of his endurance. He gasps

and Edwina pauses in her fingerings, then suddenly she rams him deeply, filling his bottomhole with three fingers. His anal ring is stretched to the limit as his penis begins the twitching. Nannette's eyes sparkle as she holds a handkerchief under his organ so his eruption will not soil the carpet. We watch his spurts spill from him and land with soft plops upon Nannette's lace handkerchief. Robert's sides are heaving and he bites his lip as Edwina's fingers probe his bottom and encourage the draining of his balls.

Charles joins us a bit later for lunch. Robert has been shut up in his room. After lunch Nannette sees to Robert's discipline and I join Charles in the study downstairs. I am completely naked. He feasts his eager eyes upon my bottomglobes and then my muff as I turn about before him.

"Nina, you must marry me! I beg you. Please consider it. I would make you a fine husband and you would be the wife of my wildest dreams."

"Oh, Charles, you are very sweet, but these things take time. First we must have a proper courtship." I kiss his cheek almost chastely. His eyes are fevered. With the wealth of Charles Evelyn Highgate behind me, the world could be my plaything. He unbuttons his trousers and takes out his weapon. I kneel naked on the floor before him. He is most swollen. I shall relieve him with my mouth. I would devour his manhood. I sit upon my bare heels and feast upon his tool. I lick about the head and nurse at him. I love the warmth of him in my mouth—the throbbing upon my tongue. From time to time I pull my lips from him and smile up at him. My hair is up in back but in my eyes in front. I suck him. My slit is very wet indeed. I tongue him madly, swirling around the slit in the head of his prick and cupping the entire helmet with my lips. When I lick up and down the shaft he fairly writhes in my grasp, a prisoner of my mouth. It is all so very, very simple! I begin to draw breath, sucking at his tool as if to vacuum the sperm from him. Charles' eyes widen. At last he moans. I tighten my lips about him and suck for all I am worth. My lips are just beyond his helmet. I savor his twitchings and hot spurtings upon my tongue. He trembles as my mouth fills with his surrender.

Charles cannot stay for dinner with us but promises to return tomorrow afternoon. He cuts a most dashing figure. Truly I shall marry him. I had so determined when I met him, yet he must pay proper court to me first. I will wait until my reins are firmly fastened on him before I assent. Then there shall be no limit to my domain. I giggle at the vision of bewhiskered lords crawling naked, swollen with arousal, at my feet.

At dinner I have poor Robert tormented yet more. He will not be allowed any more spendings while he is under my training. It will amuse me to ignore his cock's swollen and desperate pleading. It is an art to keep the male ever on the edge of spurting release. He must be teased until he is almost mad with the urge to spill his sperm...then kept there, poised on the brink of delicious solace. Women with laughing eyes and impudent hands make excellent tormentors in this respect. The male's bridle hangs helpless and silly between his legs, easy prey for soft, knowing, feminine fingers.

I have Robert led to the dinner table by his penis. Clara so enjoys this task! Then I instruct her and Belinda to bind him fast to his chair. While Nannette, Edwina and I carry on our conversation, the maids take turns feeding and tormenting Robert. Clara feeds him brimming spoonfuls of warm broth while Belinda is busy tickling his shaved genitals with teasing strokes of her fingertips. Belinda's innocent eyes sparkle and her smiles dimple her cheeks as Robert squirms unavailingly. Clara deliberately tips his spoon so the broth runs down his chin. We all laugh at his discomfiture and the maids scold him and pinch his balls. Clara soon makes him spill a bit more broth and Belinda takes his penis between her palms and yanks it soundly several times. The look of pain and ecstasy on Robert's face is simply too amusing for words!

After dinner we amuse ourselves with Robert in the study. Edwina holds a book of Virgil up before his eyes and demands he read from it, translating correctly from the Latin. Belinda stands smirking behind him with a well-oiled phallus at the ready. Clara stands by with a supple birch rod. I, of course, supervise the educational proceedings. Poor Robert begins translating from the fourth canto. His naked helplessness amuses me. He translates the verses of the fourth canto very well at first, but I sabotage his efforts.

"Belinda, please insert the phallus well into his bottom and wiggle it about. I mean this to be a lesson in concentration for him. There is scarcely any skill I know of that is more valuable than the power to concentrate."

Belinda bends down behind Robert, most eager to fulfill her intimate duties upon his person. Edwina is biting her lip in an effort not to laugh as Robert's eyes widen when the phallus is pressed firmly into him by the maid.

He hesitates in his translation and Edwina prods him to continue. With a dildo up his ass the poor boy cannot help himself and soon stumbles over the passages most miserably. I have Belinda step back from him. I tell Clara to give him a dozen firm lashes with the birch across the back of his thighs and order Robert to see that he does not expel the phallus or he will get a dozen more. The blows of correction fall and Robert whimpers. He retains the dildo. Then we have him translating again. And so it proceeds. Five laughing women tormenting a helpless male.

After we have finished our games with Robert I have the maids fasten him to his bedposts for the night. Their hands are busy beneath his nightshirt for a long while before they let him alone. His organ is gently stroked to the brink of hope and then left to throb in despair. He looks so helpless with his genitals shaved.

I have Nannette and Edwina up in my room. We three wear only tightly-laced corsets. Edwina's bottom is very fulsome and I have seen it more than once catch the eye of males on the street. Her breasts are ripe and pert with large nipples and show promise of additional filling out. She sits between Nannette and me upon the settee. I rest my fingers on her thigh and then move a bit more boldly so my hand fairly brushes the foliage of her mount. She smiles at me and blushes prettily, hoping I will continue. My fingertips soon find and caress her pussy lips and soon

I am rubbing her now-swollen clit. Nannette has her hand under Edwina's bottom and the dear girl is near to swooning with excitement. I find this multiple activity very exciting, and I caress Edwina's slit fervidly. I take her engorged clit between thumb and forefinger and rub it gently, enjoying the way the girl shudders each time I repeat the motion. Finally I move my fingers to the threshold of her womanhood and slowly cross over. I insert two of them into the slit and gently move them around, testing, stretching. Her conch-like membranes are smooth and slippery. I am encouraged to delve deeper by the way she thrusts her hips against me. I wiggle my digits and plunge them within her cunt until only my knuckles show. I keep my hand flat against her mount and pressure her while I move my fingers in and out in a steady motion. Edwina begins to thrust uncontrollably against me and spends in an uncontrollable deluge that leaves my fingers sopping.

Nannette and I bring her to orgasm several times and then Edwina graciously begins to rub my slit. The little minx wants to make me spend and indeed she shall, for I am close already. Her other hand rubs my bottom as I lay back upon the settee. Her fingers are most curious in their delvings and soon one works past my anus and probes the depths of my fundament. I whimper and spend deliciously. Through the haze of my delight I see Nannette kneeling behind Edwina, tonguing her peach with a most gentle lapping. We three are then but a tangle of busy fingers and tingling private parts upon the settee as we explore the limits of tender feminine ecstasies. Edwina smiles like a cat and begs my permission to give Robert a slow birching in the morning. The girl truly delights in cruelty. Of course I will not deny her.

As sunlight spills through Robert's window the next morning he is taken to the punishment room by the maids. There we await him. Clara and Belinda fasten him down, naked, to the punishment bench. Edwina stands ready to administer the birching as I promised her. She is naked save for a short leather apron. Whipping is very warm work and the dear girl should be attired comfortably for it. She blushes most prettily at the sight of Robert's pleading erection. Edwina then sets about flaying Robert's bottom. She has always had the instinct for such things and now she has the expertise. Her pert young breasts bounce with each hard stroke she lays upon him. The cheeks of her bottom fairly pout beneath her tight apron straps. Robert only receives one respite from his ordeal. At one point Edwina is amused because his agonized writhings make him indeed look ridiculous. She stops for a bit and giggles. Then she bends down and murmurs in his ear. "Robert, your poor cock seems in dire need of relief." She prances around behind him again; all the while his fevered eyes are upon her wiggling bottom. She raises her arched bare foot and ever-so-gently teases his prick with her coy little toes. She nudges and wiggles it until he wets himself with the precursors of spending. Then she giggles again and leaves him unsatiated.

Slowly she birches him to, and then beyond the point of endurance. She lays on the rod in broad, sweeping strokes that cross his buttocks. Then she changes the pattern and swishes from top to bottom. Finally she undercuts as best as she is able, in an effort to tickle his cock and balls. Edwina truly delights in the infliction of pain. She told me but last night, laughing as she said it—that she dreams of being the star performer in a circus of torments. To the roars and adulation of the crowd she would inflict the most frightful tortures on naked, bound males. Just in the telling, her cheeks flushed and her eyes sparkled.

I wish now to have Robert to myself for a bit. I have him naked in my dressing room, just the two of us. He is rather in awe of me and trembles as I survey him. His penis is pendant, yet slowly thickens as I take it in hand to inspect him. His bottom bears the marks of Edwina's disciplinary strokes.

I have him lie down upon my carpet. His balls being so nicely shaved, it would be a shame not to toy with them. I massage them gently and stroke his bobbing shaft at the same time. Robert so dearly wants to spend. He bites his lip as clear droplets from his cockhead wet my hands. I gently chide him for his impropriety. How he longs to be taken in hand and masturbated until he is drained and senseless. How his longing amuses me!

I wear a rubber apron. It is black, shiny, and ever-so-smooth. Robert's eyes are quite taken with it. I cannot resist. I have him up again, lying across my rubber-aproned lap. I spank his bottom with my hand. I do not have to spank him hard. He is frightfully sore from Edwina's dealings with him. His writhings, of course, rub his prick about on my rubber apron most. Alas, I do not allow him the time needed for release. I have him on the floor again, upon his back. I stand over him and lower myself down upon him. I order him to kiss my bottom. He does so with an eagerness born of an intense, almost agonized longing. I do not stop there. I make him kiss, then tongue my asshole. The sensation is delightful! I have him thrust his tongue within and wiggle it about. Robert's servile tongue soothes my fundament. I have him at it for over an hour. I spend and spend again while looking down at his penis drizzling clear drops and twitching its longing for my hands. I do not even deign to touch it. I simply wiggle my bottom greedily upon his face and spend. He gasps for breath beneath my cheeks!

I determine to put Robert further to the test. He shall be vigorously exercised while under my auspices. He shall be taken to the limits of control and even beyond. I will pronounce his training at an end when he is utterly pliable. He must be convinced once and for all as to the superiority of the fair sex. His highest dream must be to serve.

I have Nannette assist me. We are in her room. She sits naked and smiling upon her bed. Robert stands nearby with his wrists fastened together behind him. I am clad still in my rubber apron. I shall play the handmaid while Robert pleasures Nannette's bottom with his prick. She has the desire to have him in her backside. We shall not let him spend, however. He will not be allowed any relief. His control will now be put to the ultimate test.

I have him kneel up on the bed. While Nannette watches I toy with his prick, sliding his foreskin gently up and down its length. His balls hang low, full and fat. How they need the emptying they will not receive!

Nannette is on all fours upon her coverlet now, facing away from Robert. His eyes fairly stroke her curvaceous bottomcheeks with longing. I guide him forward. His balls are a leash in my hands. I steer his cockhead to her anal ring. With my other hand I slap his bottom. "Push, you silly boy! I want her bottom to feast on your prick." I watch his prick slide deeply into Nannette's bottom. Her anus clutches him tightly. Nannette wiggles her hips and their coupling is complete. I have him probe her and he does, trying feverishly to please his mistresses. Nannette's liquid moans tease his ears as her bottom torments his prick. She gasps and spends, her hole sucking upon his tool. I find that I must twist and slap his balls so that he will not ejaculate into her bottom and find release. Nannette works her butthole selfishly upon him. Her bottom swallows his tool. His eyes are haggard.

In the afternoon Charles visits us. He will bring Nannette and me to another party later in the evening. He joins us for a late luncheon. We talk of Edwina. Charles is pleased at Edwina's progress. The maids serve us in silent efficiency. Robert is shut away upstairs.

After we have finished lunch, Charles and I retire to the library. I desire the satisfaction of his tool at my rear portal once again. I find the sensation of fullness most naughty and rather exquisite.

He unbuttons his trousers and brings out his swollen ramrod for my inspection.

"Oh, Charles, it is so very swollen. I must take whatever measures are proper to relieve it." As I talk I am pumping his organ to and fro in my fist. Charles' jaw goes slack. His chest is heaving with passion. I have him quite mad with lust.

"Oh, Nina, even your hands enslave me. Stop this teasing I beg you. Soothe me with your bottom! What a cruel beauty you are, Nina. Who could ever deny you!"

I giggle and raise my skirts. I bend over at the waist, supporting myself with my hands flat against the leather bound books. My pussyslit pouts nakedly at him. My buttocks thrust outward to his enraptured gaze. I feel the heat of his tool at my bottom. First the tightness, the probing, and then the delicious slow torture of his insertion. He is in me now up to his balls. He has quite driven me up on tiptoe. I gasp at the thrusting of his turgid girth in my bottomhole. I rest my fevered cheek against the wall panel. I am flushed. My lips are parted. My bottom sucks upon his penis. I slowly bounce up and down, reveling in the sensation as my buttocks impact against Charles' thighs. I sit down hard upon him and wriggle my bottom around, his swollen tool embedded deeply. I examine his face. He is flushed and transfixed. He is thoroughly in my power. I begin pumping his tool mercilessly with my bottom. Charles moans and I feel his twitching and then the warmth of his spurting deep in my bottom. I have quelled him once again. My bottom has mastered him.

CHAPTER VIII

The party is at a fine home belonging to the Earl of Brighton. There are dozens of guests. It is an exclusive affair. I whisper to Nannette, "Think of all the power, wealth and influence represented here. One has only to control the penises of the men who wield the power and one has everything."

Nannette laughs at my observations. When Percy is back with her he will be but a puppet under her thumb!

I am clad in black and lavender with a bodice cut low enough to attract interest, yet not cause scandal. I wear a nosegay of bright blue flowers, given me by Charles. We circulate with the other guests through the sumptuous drawing rooms. Charles introduces me to many of his friends. One stately Baroness places her gloved hand upon my arm. "You know, he is in love with you dear. We all talk of it. I believe if you look down at your little finger you will find him there twisted about it. It is most excellent. You come from a fine family. I think you shall be good for him." I thank her and blush most graciously with a hint of shyness. I modestly lower my eyes.

I even see some old friends of my family in the company of guests. The attitude here is one of acceptance. One who is in the least bit questionable would have received no invitation at all. Men look at me with hungry eyes. How I know their weaknesses! If their glances hold my eyes too long I flush and turn away. Stern old members of the nobility with their voices talking of empire and glory would like nothing more than to be naked at my feet. I have toyed with such before. I have had them kneeling and licking between my toes while I assumed an expression of languid boredom and disinterest. Their organs—usually limp—swell to hugeness under the lash of my tongue. Such men have been known to spill their sperm just from the rapture they feel at a pretty woman's angry tirade.

Nannette attracts her share of interested male admirers. She has become adept at handling them. Her laughter teases them, yet keeps them helplessly at arm's length.

A tall young man tries successfully to engage me in conversation. We talk of the paintings of Auguste Renoir. The young man tells me that he believes Renoir will achieve fame well beyond his century.

"Are you familiar with his latest work, 'Luncheon Of The Boating Party?'" he inquires.

"Yes, I believe so. I have seen it in exhibit."

"Permit me the impropriety, yet I must say you do remind me of the young woman holding up the little dog. I cannot help but envy him. To be held up and admonished affectionately by such as you...I would gladly give up my manhood and take up the form of a beast."

I laugh at him. This one amuses me. He no doubt would gladly give up his manhood. But he would, I am sure, prefer to give it up in the form of thick spurts of his passion potion spilling into my teasing hand. "I am sure you would be very unhappy as my beast," I tease. "What if I should never have you over upon your back to gently caress your belly. What if I should rather take you to be gelded for my idle convenience and beat you if you displeased me?" My eyes and voice mock him, yet he is undaunted.

"These things would be an easy price to pay for the honor of fawning at your feet." His eyes are upon my breasts now.

I giggle in spite of myself. I cannot help it. Games with such as he are most amusing. I continue to play with him. "Do you not suppose that the poor crew of Odysseus tired of their animal status under the cruel dominion of Circe?" I ask. I lower my voice. "I am sure when they grovelled before her, swollen with adoration, that it only amused her. No doubt she laughed at their anguish. Perhaps she allowed her maids to toy with them and let them find release in their lewd, uncaring hands."

His cheeks redden at my insinuations. He blushes at my effrontery. "I confess, I have always found the story of Circe most fascinating. Were I Odysseus I would drain the enchanted cup so that I might forever be her beast. I can think of no fairer fate to befall me."

Nannette joins us now and we three find a quiet corner. We are sheltered from the other guests by a screened balustrade and the foliage of an exotic plant. Charles has been occupied elsewhere. I smile at Nannette. "This one longs to be a naked beast serving at the feet of Circe. Isn't it amusing!"

Nannette surveys him disdainfully. He swallows hard. "Were I Circe and were he my beast I would lash him most properly for his impertinence."

I smile at him and goad him further. "Would you not even caress him if the strokes of his servile tongue upon your person brought you satisfaction, Nannette?" I ask innocently.

"I should never do other than rule over him with cruelty," Nannette declares.

I reach out and gently rub the front of his trousers. "I should caress my beast like this from time to time, though I should beat him often as well," I purr.

I busy my hands undoing his trouser buttons and withdrawing his tool. I handle him easily and find him most helpless in my grasp. Nannette is playing along with my little game. She plays merciless foil to my kinder role. I extract his balls and leave them to dangle against his trouser front while I begin working his prick. It is long and thin and possessed of a head that seems far too large for its shaft. He burns in my hand and grows rock-hard. I smile up into his face. I have him facing the corner. My fist exercises him most diligently. "Nannette, he is going to spend! Please prepare to catch his sperm in your hand. We mustn't have him soiling the floor of this splendid place."

Nannette obliges me and cups her palm beneath the tip of his tool. With a strangled groan he erupts into her hand, filling her palm with his sperm. We laugh at him. Nannette rubs his sperm upon the front of his trousers, then we take our leave of him. He is wide-eyed and gasping at both the condition of his diminishing prick and the condition of his trousers.

A group of ladies soon collects in a more intimate drawing room, smaller than the rest. Nannette and I join readily in the conversation and the mood is relaxed and brimming with amusement. Quiet servants pass through our midst with silver trays upon which stand elegant crystal glasses full of spirits. The group becomes closed to males. Even the boldest male who comes near is turned away by glances that are not welcoming and the sudden hush in our conversation that lasts until he retreats. Women often form such alliances with each other. Males cannot do so, however, as they are but strutting peacocks, fluffing their plumes in hope of catching the female's eye. Each is so jealous of the other. How they amuse us!

The conversation unfolds with a forthrightness and intimacy that would be impossible elsewhere. Our settees are arranged in a close circle and the sherry is relaxing us. The result is that we are surprisingly candid and not a little risque. One pretty young woman relates a tale of a suitor that she once had who was most fascinated with her feet. I catch Nannette's eye and she smiles at me. Our games with the man who wanted but to be the beast of Circe are an ideal compliment to this turn of topic. The woman is urged by her friends to explain what she meant in greater detail.

"Well, when we prepared for a fox hunt he would often look longingly at my black riding boots the whole while. He told me that he admired the glint of my spurs and the swell of my calves in the tight leather. I thought him a trifle silly perhaps, yet harmless on the whole. When I wore my fine bench-crafted dress boots he was always intrigued as well. One afternoon, though, I came to be quite disgusted with him."

She wishes to bring her story to an end here, but we will not hear of it. We press her eagerly to continue. We are all itching for the scandal of every intriguing detail. Somewhat reluctantly, yet with a smile, she continues.

"One afternoon, I was rather warm and I removed my boots and pulled up my skirts just a bit to refresh myself. He and I were alone in my drawing room. He actually trembled at the sight of my silk-stockinged feet. He begged, even pleaded with me to be allowed to rub them. I assented finally to quiet him down. I assumed he hoped for a glimpse of my thighs, or even…well, you know. Anyway, he moved nearer to me upon the settee and I placed my feet in his lap. He rubbed them for a bit and then without warning he began covering them with passionate kisses. He pressed his nose and lips to my stockinged toes like he was famished and they could satiate him. What disgusted me, however, was the protuberance in the crotch of his trousers! I had never seen the like of it! As I watched in disdain I saw it twitch beneath the fabric of his trousers and suddenly his trousers were spotted by something wet from beneath. And this before he even attempted to see my thighs and mount! You may be sure I had my servants escort him out forthwith and he was never welcome again. Of this you may be certain!"

The room erupts in laughter at the conclusion of her account. We all agree that males are most loathsome when left to their own devices and need to be firmly taken in hand. Disdain and curiosity are two emotions never far apart when one talks of male propensities.

Another lady tells of a pretty young governess she retained who came to her with excellent references. "She would not, however, relate to me the reason for which she left her previous employer," said the woman, while we paid rapt attention. "I pressed her hard for the details and at last she relented and told me. She had been placed in charge of a boy who was most recalcitrant and perhaps too old to be given over to a governess. The lad fancied himself in love with her.

"The lad's behavior around her became more and more unusual. She disciplined him severely but seemingly to no avail. About this time she began to notice that her most dainty dress shoes were often slightly wet. She was at a loss to explain this phenomenon. One afternoon, she determined to fully investigate the matter. She made her charge understand that she would be out for quite some time. He believed himself to be solely in the care of the cook, who had no interest in his doings and let him run about unimpeded. The charming young governess left her shoes upon the carpet in her chamber beside her bed. She quietly hid herself in a linen closet down the hall and waited. Soon she heard footfalls passing the closet door and entering her room. When her door was shut she crept from her hiding place and tiptoed to it. There she peeped through the keyhole to avail herself of what was going on within."

We are all fairly breathless now. The lady has our complete and total attention. We are all ears for every sordid detail of what is to follow. She surveys us with a smugness born of the realization that her audience hangs on her every word. "She saw a most disgusting and ludicrous sight! There on her carpet knelt the boy, totally naked. His clothes were scattered from the door to where he knelt as if he could not restrain himself in his excitement. He was kneeling there holding one of her dainty shoes to his lips and licking it. With his other hand he was abusing himself frantically. She watched as his stroking of himself became more vigorous and he spent in thick arcs of whiteness across the floor. The girl could not contain her indignation a moment more and entered the room to soundly thrash the naked lad. That very night she tendered her resignation!"

"I am so glad the poor girl's shoes were only moistened from the lad's worshipful tongue!" exclaims Nannette to everyone's amusement.

A petite blonde adds, "One cannot help but hope she did not spank him across her lap after his so recent a discharge!" Again there is laughter. The pretty blonde continues with a narrative of her own.

"I was once acquainted with a young governess who spanked her charge while he squatted 'bottomless' on the floor of his room. She punished him most admirably. Yet from time to time the lad spontaneously twitched to full hardness and shot his sperm upon the floor, much to her chagrin. She devised an elegantly simple remedy for this happening. She manually stimulated him to erectness before his spanking and then placed a small bottle over the tip of his cock. The vacuum from the bottle sucking at his prick kept him swollen and provided its own tight and snug fit as it were. From then on if he spilled his seed there would be no mess and no soiling of the carpet."

We all marvel at the ingeniousness of this solution.

Another pretty woman relates the story of what transpired during a painting class when she attended an exclusive school for girls in the Cotswolds. "This one bright morning, the headmistress gave us the assignment of painting a nude male. The groundskeeper was a splendid specimen and she fairly bullied him into being our naked model. You can imagine where the eyes of over a dozen young girls lingered! Inevitably the poor fellow's meat began to swell and the room erupted in giggling. The headmistress was in quite a conundrum. At last she stepped up to the fellow and took firm purchase on his prick there on the stool upon which he sat before us all. Then she set about quickly masturbating him. She was quite expert. She drew her hand up and down along his length almost impatiently, intent on returning to more important business. We watched raptly as the thick pole lengthened and became even wider around. The head seemed to balloon and assume an angry color. This encouraged the headmistress to pump him all the harder until he began to gasp and squirm upon the stool. Finally, his tool began to twitch and a thick stream of sperm erupted from the tip in several torrid bubbling gouts. She caught his effusion in her handkerchief and told us to continue as though nothing had happened. We were all abuzz with talk of this incident for days!"

There are scandalized "Ohs" and "Ahs" at the conclusion of this merry anecdote.

Another young woman tells a tale that has us all ears in no time whatever. "In my youth it was customary for us all to gather together on our family estate in Nottinghamshire. There were over a dozen cousins as well as many aunts and uncles. Two of my female cousins were very pretty and slightly older than I. I was always tagging about behind them attempting to follow their example in all that they did—or almost all that they did—as you shall soon see. I begged them to tell me where they went every morning as they tiptoed quietly from our room. They were obviously trying to do so in secret. At last they condescended to take me along after making me swear that I would not utter a word of what was to transpire.

"We tiptoed quietly to a small room where one of our male cousins lay sleeping. My two female cousins crept quietly to his bed and drew down the coverlet. He was sleeping soundly on his back. They stealthily drew up his nightshirt and exposed to my amazed view his bare privates!"

Laughter sounds about our circle at these youthful—

and in a way almost innocent—goings on. "His prick was very large," our storyteller continues, "even in its semi-soft state. His balls hung naked and low beneath it most lusciously. My cousins wasted no time and began diddling him most avidly and stifling their giggles. He never once woke, though he stirred and moaned in his sleep as though he were having an erotic dream. At last he spent copiously all over his belly while the lewd young hands of his female cousins worked him to emptiness. He shuddered and lay still, breathing deeply. I crept out followed by his two giggling masturbatrixes. When we regained our room they laughed and told me that they did it to him very early every morning. The poor lad was no doubt mystified upon awakening to find himself soiled with his own sperm each day."

Even this carnal tale is quickly upstaged. Another wealthy woman relates an erotic account of past goings on. The sherry is most excellent and we are all willing listeners.

"I also have a story to tell concerning older female cousins. When we visited my aunt, her two daughters often took me boating on the Evenlode above Swinford. They, of course, deigned not to pole our vessel, preferring instead the procurement of this service from one of the older male servants who was excused from his usual duties for the afternoon. My cousins paid no homage to his pride or dignity. As soon as we were out of sight they usually made him remove all the clothing from below his waist. Then they fixed a length of mooring cord about his cock! They sat in comfort with their shoes off and skirts drawn up—sometimes allowing their bare little cunts to show—though they were still properly hatted and gloved. They laughed at the servant and commanded him in his poling by means of tugs upon the mooring cord.

"I must say, at my impressionable age I was both repelled and fascinated by this unique sport. Two tugs meant pole left, three tugs meant pole right. A sharp series of tugs meant go faster. A slow series of tugs meant pole slower. A single tug indicated stop. My cousins delighted in the pullings and tuggings and the poor old servant poled us in circles for quite some time in following their commands. His organ was always erect and he was in a most precarious state of near-orgasm. The smirking girls frequently ordered him then to stand thrusting his prick over the side of the boat. Then they giggled madly and yanked the mooring cord until the poor fellow trembled and spurted into the Evenlode the carelessly wasted fruit of his loins. His pretty young tormentors gave him no respite and again ordered him about his poling duties in a most rude and uncaring fashion. He was upbraided for his lechery and both my cousins pronounced him disgusting."

Laughter resounds at the finish of this anecdote. It is almost time to leave the party as it is winding down. There is time for but one more tale.

A woman tells us of once spying upon her uncle when he amused himself with two of his housemaids. She was young enough at the time she witnessed their indoor sport to not fully understand its meaning, but nonetheless she realized that it was very naughty indeed.

Her uncle stood naked between the pretty housemaids who were themselves fully clothed in their black cotton uniforms decked with white lace. The maid behind her uncle was smartly slapping his bare buttocks with the flat of her hand. She had her sleeve drawn up and, healthy young girl that she was, applied great force to the blows. Her uncle's penis was of the most huge proportions one could ever imagine. It was being lasciviously licked by the second housemaid—a pretty young girl—who knelt on the floor before him. She did not apply her hands to his tool in any way, but rather kept them firmly on her hips. She licked about the head of his shaft with evident relish and then at last took it in her mouth and began to suck upon it. She licked the enormous shaft up and down, lingering at the balls, and seemed to pay special attention to the head. The maid had a very pretty mouth and her lips obviously caused him the most poignant sensations. The maid who spanked her uncle forced his prick more firmly into the other maid's throat with every blow. The spanking and the pleasurable sucking continued for a long while. At last her uncle moaned and the force of the blows upon his bottom became hard enough to drive him up on tiptoe, imbedding him sweetly in the depths of the lewd mouth that sucked him. She saw her uncle's eyes twitch shut and his jaw hang slack as the maid kneeling before him sucked all the more greedily upon his tool. The perplexed girl then saw the maid act as though she were swallowing mouthful after mouthful of something—though she could not tell what. The greedy bitch then licked her lips and wiggled her bottom as she sat back on her heels as if hoping for more, while her uncle sagged weakly to one side.

That concludes our tale-telling. We are all most scandalized. Even proper and well-bred women enjoy such tales if they are told when the time is right! We join up again with Charles, say our goodbyes and take our leave. The carriage ride home is merry. We are all in good humor. Charles sees Nannette and me to the door of Charingate House and promises to return early tomorrow.

Nannette and I enter the house and find Edwina smirking. She and the maids have been playing the most cruel and naughty games with Robert.

"He is so very silly," Edwina purrs. "One must wonder if he even has a spine at all. One can do whatever one likes with him. He is a servant, a pet, and a toy all rolled up into one!"

Nannette follows me up the stairs and into Robert's room. I want to see the aftermath of their games with him. Edwina assures me that they did not let him spend, though it took a good deal of skill to avoid this considering the excitable state he was in.

Poor Robert is tied naked to one of his bedposts. He looks wan and weak though his tool is still swollen to most respectable proportions. "Look, Nannette! They have well-whipped his thighs, both front and back, and his poor bottom as well!"

"Oh, how sweet, Nina! They have left him covered with welts and all fiery red."

They have also rubbed his tool with some sort of hot liniment that still causes him the most exquisite discomfort judging from the way he writhes and squirms against his bonds.

We laugh as we move closer to inspect him. His thighs

are moistened with his excited drippings though not with any trace of his actual sperm. They have spent hours masturbating him. How he must have moaned and pleaded for release. How they must have giggled at his tormented anguish!

Nannette and I take turns playing with his tool for a bit. Robert begs us to stop but we only laugh at him. Nannette prissily weighs his balls upon her impudent palm. She giggles and tells me that they are swollen with a great build up of joy-juice.

"Ooh, poor boy," I coo. "Do your plums need emptying so very badly? Two proper ladies such as we would never do such a wicked thing." We laugh and leave him to his misery. He shall be left there all night. Little does he know that his training is almost at an end. He will make an amusing plaything for women for years to come.

Nannette and I make plans concerning her future. According to letters from Jane, dear Percy has suffered much under her and Mary. Nannette will have no difficulty mastering him. She plans to return home and rule her household as Jane and I have ruled ours. She will make a fine mistress. She is truly spirited and most imaginative. No male who has been slowly drawn to spurting in her hands has ever forgotten the addictive pleasure of it. Even Sir Albert is sometimes known to spill his seed when she but reaches for his tool. Of course he is upbraided soundly for his lack of self-control.

Charles is true to his word. Early the next morning he is at my door and the maids admit him. He is very earnest and asks if we might retire upstairs to my drawing room. I well know what is coming. Males are so predictable as to be boring at times. Charles can be sweet, but he lacks imagination. Of course, what he lacks in imagination is more than made up for by his vast fortune. I feel his eyes upon the swell of my calves as he follows me up the carpeted steps. How the calves, ankles and feet of a pretty woman enslave the imagination of many males. One can so easily lure them to any degradation!

When we reach my drawing room Charles becomes nervous. At last he seems to take himself in hand. He has me sit in an armchair and gets down upon his knees before me. He raises my hand to his lips and kisses it. He reaches beneath his waistcoat and withdraws a small velvet box. He presents it to me.

"Nina, I beg you. Please marry me! I must have you! I am fairly mad with love and desire." He pauses while I smile teasingly at him. "Please, Nina, open the box. I do hope you like it."

I open the box. I do like it! The ring fairly dazzles me. It is a masterpiece. It is quite literally crusted with diamonds and topped with a large, brilliantly flawless stone! I pretend disappointment, as if I have hoped for more. I hesitate. Charles leans forward and throws his arms about my knees. He looks up imploringly into my eyes. I keep him on edge a few moments more. At last I pretend to relent. I nod. I say I will marry him. He nearly sobs with relief and joy.

Charles rises to his feet and kisses me. He laughs like a schoolboy. To have such power over another is a heady amusement.

I stand up. I press myself against him as we kiss. I feel his organ swell beneath his clothing. He begs for my mouth upon his tool. He has the desire to feel my lips upon him and have me swallow his come as he spends. I coolly decline. Instead I reach out and undo his trouser buttons. I bring forth his tool. I grip it tightly, clutching it with my fingernails, and work it up and down. He gasps my name and spurts almost immediately into my hand. I smile as I watch his sperm drip through my fingers and onto the patterned carpet. How weak my hand has made him! I could ask anything of him and it would be granted me.

I stand with his shrinking and submissive organ in one hand and his balls in the other. I smile sweetly up at him. The world is truly at my feet!

OTHER BOOKS AVAILABLE FROM MASQUERADE'S EROTIC LIBRARY...

PAUL LITTLE

RED DOG SALOON **68-8** **$4.95**
Quantrill's Raiders pillaged Kansas during the Civil War. Belle Denburg took a vow to avenge one of their victims, her cousin Genevieve, kidnapped and I raped. Belle intended to get herself accepted as a camp follower to Quantrill, find the men responsible and kill them. Her pursuit led her through whore houses, rapes, and tar-and-featherings until at last, unsuspecting, she held each of the guilty ones between her legs. Lust and revenge!

PASSION IN RIO **54-8** **$4.95**
"There is a very rich man who is a photographer," he said shifting his eyes nervously, "he wishes to have a North American woman pose for him. He will tie you up and make you wear a costume such as prisoners wore many hundreds of years ago. And for this he will pay a great deal of money. Will you do that?"

LUST OF THE COSSACKS **41-6** **$4.95**
The carriage stopped in front of the house and Vassili, who was first to open the door, bowed his head low in homage to his young master, "Welcome, master," he said humbly. Piotor Kalinnikoff, in his resplendent captain's uniform, smiled and turned to Olga: "You see how I'm thought of here, my beauty," he chuckled. "You'll have more attention here than at the Czar's own court, and the command performances will be much more exciting!"

LISETTE JOYAUX **10-6** **$4.75**
An innocent maid falls into a nest of lesbians. The four lovely ladies overpower and explore her. They stimulate every opening in her body, sucking her sweet virginal nectar. To their delight, she returns their caresses with a licking lust that exceeds their own. They have awakened a ferocious lesbian appetite. After she marries, the lusty lesbians kidnap the young bride for some more Sapphic savagery. Fiery French perversions!

THE SLAVES OF CAMEROON **49-1** **$4.95**
This sordid tale set during the German occupation of Cameroon, is about the women who were used by German officers for salacious profit. These women were forced to become whores for the German army in this African colony. The most perverse forms of erotic gratification are depicted in this unsavory tale!

THE TEARS OF THE INQUISITION **34-3** **$4.95**
"Even now, in mortal terror, Rosanna's nakedness reminded her of her happily married nights. There was a tickling inside her as her nervous system reminded her that she was ready for sex. But before her was a man for whom she could feel only the most deeply rooted horror—the Inquisitor!"

THE NUNNERY TALES 20-3 $4.95

Innocent novices are helpless in the hands of corrupt clerics. The Abbess forces her rites of sexual initiation on any maiden who falls into her hands. Father Abelard delivers his penance with smart strokes of the whip on his female penitents' bottoms. After exposure to the Mother Superior and her lustful nuns, sweet Emilie, Louise, and the other novices are sexual novices no longer. Cloistered concubinage!

PLEASURES AND FOLLIES 26-2 $4.95

The Erotikon of an English libertine. "I got astride her, rode her roughshod, plied the crop...Ashamed by these excesses provoked by my reading, I compiled a well-seasoned Erotikon and it excited me to such a degree that I...well, pick up my book, gentle reader, and you'll see whether it has a similar effect upon you."

AUTOBIOGRAPHY OF A FLEA II 07-6 $4.75

The world-famous flea journeys to France where he continues to pen his observations on female sexual foibles from his special vantage points. The buttocks of busty, lusty Dame Lucille; the love nest of luscious soon—to-be-ex-virgin Laurette. And between the breasts of Madame Bernard, who longs for the nine inch penance that lies beneath sly Père Mourier's cassock. A real French tickler!

FRUITS OF PASSION 05-X $4.75

A classic study of Victorian sexual obsession. From his initiation into endless orgiastic delights by the slippery lips of the chambermaid sisters, Rose and Manette, the Count de Leon continues his erotic diary for forty years, ending with his Caribbean voyages with the two most uninhibited Victorian Venuses he has ever known. A life totally dedicated to sex!

STUDENTS OF PASSION 22-X $4.95

When she arrives at the prestigious Beauchampe Academy, Francine is young, innocent, and eager to learn. But her daily lessons have nothing to do with grammar and spelling. Her teachers and schoolmates enroll her in a course devoted to passion, anatomy, and lust...and she's determine to graduate with honors.

ALEXANDER TROCCHI

THONGS 46-7 $4.95

Spain, perhaps more than any other country in the world, is the land of passion and of death. And in Spain life is cheap, from that glittering tragedy in the bullring to the quick thrust of the stiletto in a narrow street in a Barcelona slum. No, this death would not have called for further comment had it not been for one striking fact. The naked woman had met her end in a way he had never seen before—a way that had enormous sexual significance. My God, she had been...

MY LIFE AND LOVES (THE 'LOST' VOLUME) 52-1 $4.95

What happens when you try to fake a sequel to the most scandalous autobiography of the 20th century? If the "forgers" are two of the most important figures in modern Erotica, you get a masterpiece, and THIS IS IT!

THE CARNAL DAYS OF HELEN SEFERIS 35-1 $4.95

"Ahmed will show you where to go," I said softly in her ear. She froze momentarily, hesitated, and then got up and mechanically turned to follow him. I couldn't be sure she knew what she was going for, that is to say, what beyond the amorphous, the unknown...Except that she knew she was being involved in some vast sexual trauma of her own choosing. Soon, though, she would assert the direction of her own lust.

HELEN AND DESIRE 65-3 $4.95

Helen Seferis's flight from the oppressive village of her birth became a sexual tour of the world of white slavery. She was held captive in a brothel for women in Sidney. In Singapore, she fell into the hands of the master of the drug trade. She escaped to Algiers where she became part of a sheik's harem. He handed her over to a white slave caravan. Helen's responses to her sexual adventures are detailed with great sensitivity in her diary. Adventurous, erotic and insightful—a marvellous book!

YOUNG ADAM 63-7 $4.95

Two British barge operators discover a girl drowned in the river Clyde. Her lover, a plumber, is arrested for her murder. But he is innocent. Joe, the barge assistant, knows that. As the plumber is tried and sentenced to hang, this knowledge lends poignancy to his romances with the women along the river whom he will love then...well, read on.

THE MASQUERADE CLASSIC EROTIC BIOGRAPHIES

THE MISFORTUNES OF MARY 27-0 $4.95

Mary came from her uncle's parsonage in Ireland to be a writer's assistant in London, in response to an ad run in the Gazette by Mrs. Coates. But the lady was a procuress, and the writer was a libertine who paid a hundred pounds for Mary's virginity. As he broke her in, Mrs. Coates sold spectator seats in her secret viewing room to Lord Strongcock and his two randy friends. Then she sold the no-longer-virginal Mary to them. White hot white slavery!

EVELINE 14-9 $4.95

Oh, that Eveline! "My dress was well open in front. His hand still lingered on my knee, on the silk stocking around which I sought to clasp my garter. I kissed him warmly on the lips. He pushed the tip of his hot tongue into my mouth. My tongue met his." Nobody in England was as hot as Eveline!

PAULINE 09-2 $4.95

From rural America to the Frankfurt Opera House to the royal court of Austria, Pauline follows her ever growing sexual desires. "They knew not that I was a prima donna, sought after by royalty, indulged and petted by the elite of all Europe. I would never see them again. Why shouldn't I give myself to them that they might become more and more inspired to deeds of greater lust!"

A Complete Listing Of MASQUERADE'S EROTIC LIBRARY

THE MEMOIRS OF MADELEINE	01-7	$4.75
SECRETS OF THE CITY	03-3	$4.75
LOVE'S ILLUSION	06-8	$4.75
ANNABEL FANE	08-4	$4.75
FRUITS OF PASSION	05-X	$4.75
THE FURTHER ADVENTURES OF MADELEINE	04-1	$4.75
PAULINE	09-2	$4.95
THE METAMORPHOSIS OF LISETTE JOYAUX	10-6	$4.75
THE YELLOW ROOM	02-5	$4.75
AUTOBIOGRAPHY OF A FLEA II	07-6	$4.75
MAN WITH A MAID	15-7	$4.75
PLAYGIRL FANTASIES	13-0	$4.75
CAPTIVE MAIDENS	12-2	$4.95
THE EROTIC READER	11-4	$4.95
EVELINE	14-9	$4.95
SLAVE ISLAND	19-X	$4.95
THE EROTIC READER VOL 2	18-1	$4.95
DARLING/INNOCENCE	24-6	$4.95
THE PRODIGAL VIRGIN	23-8	$4.95
THE GILDED LILY	25-4	$4.95
PLEASURES AND FOLLIES	26-2	$4.95
STUDENTS OF PASSION	22-X	$4.95
THE STORY OF HOLLYWOOD O	16-5	$4.95
THE MISFORTUNES OF MARY	27-0	$4.95
THE NUNNERY TALES	20-3	$4.95
THE LUSTFUL TURK	28-9	$4.95
DEVA-DASI	29-7	$4.95
THE STORY OF MONIQUE	42-4	$4.95
THE ENGLISH GOVERNESS	43-2	$4.95
POOR DARLINGS	33-5	$4.95
DANGEROUS LESSONS	32-7	$4.95
DANCE HALL GIRLS	44-0	$4.95
LAVENDER ROSE	30-0	$4.95

KAMA HOURI	39-4	$4.95
THONGS	46-7	$4.95
THE PLEASURE THIEVES	36-X	$4.95
THE TEARS OF THE INQUISITION	34-3	$4.95
SACRED PASSIONS	21-1	$4.95
THE DISCIPLINE OF ODETTE	47-5	$4.95
THE CARNAL DAYS OF HELEN SEFERIS	35-1	$4.95
LUST OF THE COSSACKS	41-6	$4.95
THE DELICIOUS DAUGHTER	53-X	$4.95
THE JAZZ AGE	48-3	$4.95
THE SLAVES OF CAMEROON	49-1	$4.95
HOUSES OF JOY	51-3	$4.95
MY LIFE AND LOVES (THE LOST VOLUME)	52-1	$4.95
PASSION IN RIO	54-8	$4.95
RAWHIDE LUST	55-6	$4.95
LUSTY LESSONS	31-9	$4.95
FESTIVAL OF VENUS	37-8	$4.95
INTIMATE PLEASURES	38-6	$4.95
TURKISH DELIGHTS	40-8	$4.95
THE KING OF PLEASURE	45-9	$4.95
JADE EAST	60-2	$4.95
BUSINESS AS USUAL	56-4	$4.95
CHINESE JUSTICE AND OTHER STORIES	57-2	$4.95
A WEEKEND VISIT	59-9	$4.95
TICKLED PINK	58-0	$4.95
KIM'S PASSION	50-5	$4.95
THE EROTIC ADV. OF HARRY TEMPLE	62-9	$4.95
YOUNG ADAM	63-7	$4.95
CLAUDINE	64-5	$4.95
HELEN AND DESIRE	65-3	$4.95
PLEASURE OF PRIVATE EYE	66-1	$4.95
MORE EROTIC ADV. OF HARRY TEMPLE	67-X	$4.95
RED DOG SALOON	68-8	$4.95
MORE PLAYGIRL FANTASIES	69-6	$4.95
NINA FOXTON	70-X	$4.95
DIARY OF AN ANGEL	71-8	$4.95
HAREM SONG	73-4	$4.95
KATY'S AWAKENING	74-2	$4.95
CELESTE	75-0	$4.95
ANGELA	76-9	$4.95
THE END OF INNOCENCE	77-7	$4.95

ORDERING IS EASY!

MC/VISA ORDERS CAN BE PLACED BY CALLING OUR TOLL-FREE NUMBER

1-800-458-9640

OR MAIL THE COUPON BELOW TO:
MASQUERADE BOOKS
801 SECOND AVE.,
NEW YORK, N.Y. 10017

70-X

QTY	TITLE	No.	PRICE
	SUBTOTAL		
	POSTAGE and HANDLING		
	TOTAL		

Add $1.00 Postage and Handling for first book and .50 cents for each additional book. Outside the U.S. add $2.00 for first book, $1.00 for each additional book. New York state residents add 81/4% sales tax.

NAME ____________________

ADDRESS ____________________ **APT #** ________

CITY ____________ **STATE** __________ **ZIP** ____________

TEL (**)** ____________________

PAYMENT: ☐ **CHECK** ☐ **MONEY ORDER** ☐ **VISA** ☐ **MC**

CARD NO. ____________________ **EXP. DATE** ____________

PLEASE ALLOW **4-6 WEEKS** DELIVERY. NO C.O.D. ORDERS. PLEASE MAKE ALL CHECKS PAYABLE TO MASQUERADE BOOKS. PAYABLE IN U.S. CURRENCY ONLY.